## 'Your wife! *Your wife!*'

Stephanie exploded in a furious whisper, then continued, 'I'd sooner be introduced as a nymphomaniacal axe murderer! At least *that* would leave me with some dignity and credibility!'

'Cut the theatrics, Steff,' Jye told her firmly. 'We've got to get our story straight.'

'*Our* story! You want me to expose myself to public ridicule and pretend I'm married to you?'

'A lot of women happen to think I qualify as a terrific catch…'

**Alison Kelly**, a self-confessed sports junkie, plays netball, volleyball and touch football, and lives in Australia's Hunter Valley. She has three children and the type of husband women tell their daughters doesn't exist in real life! He's not only a better cook than Alison, but he isn't afraid of vacuum cleaners, washing machines or supermarkets. Which is just as well, otherwise this book would have been written by a starving woman in a pigsty!

**Recent titles by the same author:**

MAN ABOUT THE HOUSE

# THE MARRIAGE ASSIGNMENT

### BY
### ALISON KELLY

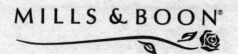

MILLS & BOON®

*First published in Great Britain 1998*
*Harlequin Mills & Boon Limited,*
*Eton House, 18-24 Paradise Road, Richmond, Surrey TW9 1SR*

© Alison Kelly 1998

ISBN 0 263 81439 4

*Set in Times Roman 10 on 10½ pt.*
*01-9901-59443 C1*

*Printed and bound in Norway*
*by AIT Trondheim AS, Trondheim*

# CHAPTER ONE

THE door of Jye's office burst open so violently he half expected to find a fully armed SWAT team storming the room; instead it was a five-foot-four platinum blonde in a canary-yellow suit.

'G'day Steff,' he said, setting aside the report he'd been reviewing. 'Duncan said you were back.'

'He knew!' she responded by way of a greeting.

*Oh, oh,* Jye thought, belatedly yearning for the SWAT team. Stephanie Worthington in a snit wasn't something a man should have to handle without at least one Scotch under his belt and another in his hand. The way Steff could vacillate between volatility and vulnerability, just conversing with her on the weather could leave a person with emotional whiplash.

'Can you believe it?' she demanded. 'He's known all along he was married! I mean, he *knew* and never said a word! Oh, God! I'm so angry I could chew his heart out! I just wasn't prepared for him to drop it on me like that. Even now I can't quite believe it's happened, and—'

'Stephanie,' he cut in, recognising she was sufficiently agitated that if he didn't cut to the chase right now her ambiguous ranting might well go on for an hour without him gaining any further enlightenment. '*What* are you talking about? *Who* knew?'

'Godfather, of course.' She paced the length of his desk, fingering her short silver hair into agitated disarray. 'He's known all along he was married and *I* didn't even find out until last night! Just like that...' She snapped her fingers. 'He ups and gets married without a word!'

Anyone who didn't know Duncan Porter, would have thought his goddaughter's obvious upset at learning she was the last to hear of his marriage was understandable.

Jye, however, *did* know Duncan Porter. The man was also his guardian and had raised him from the age of ten. Which would have been challenging enough for any bachelor, even without the additional trials of raising the irate, arm-waving blonde currently speed-walking back and forth across Jye's office.

'I mean, *can you believe it*?' she repeated, giving him only a cursory glance.

Jye couldn't. The notion that seventy-two-year-old Duncan had married, *without a word to either of them*, was incomprehensible. No, make that *impossible*; it was Stephanie who was incomprehensible.

'Well, damn it, Jye!' she huffed. 'Aren't you going to say *anything*? I could use a bit of sympathy here.'

'Sorry,' he murmured, struggling to contain a grin. 'I promise to be profusely sympathetic if you'll calm down and tell me what the hell you're talking about.'

'I'm talking about Brad Carey!' Her tone and impatient look indicated the name should mean something to him.

'Carey… Carey…' The name was vaguely familiar, but— 'Ah! You mean the bloke Duncan promoted to Manager of Resort Design a week or so ago?'

A heavy sigh and a rueful nod confirmed he'd correctly identified the man. The design department wasn't Jye's usual stamping ground, and on the rare occasions he had to deal with it he did so via the manager, but as yet he and Carey had had no need for interaction.

'Well?' he prodded, when Steff continued to offer nothing more than a woebegone expression. 'What about him?'

'I just told you,' she said flatly. *'He got married.'*

'Then he's the one who needs my sympathy, not you.' Such a comment usually would have provoked one of Steff's pro-marriage lectures; instead all it produced was a tightly pursed mouth and the furious blinking of too bright eyes.

'Steff? What's up?'

'He married Karrie Dent!'

Again Jye had to struggle to put a face with the name. 'Eh...his assistant?'

'Yes!' she snapped, before moving into another head-shaking routine. 'The whole idea is *insane*. I mean, can you believe he actually married her?'

'Well, I guess she always struck me as more the career-orientated type than the executive's missus,' he offered, since it was clear Stephanie wanted his opinion. 'But she's not a bad looker, so—'

'Jye!' She shot him an *'are you a complete imbecile?'* look. 'They only got married so Brad could get the promotion!' Her tone was all disapproval and indignation. 'It's what's known as a marriage of convenience.'

'*A marriage of convenience...*' Jye laughed. 'Now *there's* an oxymoron.'

'The only *moron* is you!' she retorted, before mumbling what might have been an apology and drawing a steadying breath. 'In case you haven't realised it, *I* don't see this as a joking matter.'

'Obviously. But from where I'm sitting, as long as it's not my marriage, kiddo, it doesn't rank up there as the end of the world.'

'You don't understand!' This time both hands reached to further disturb what Jye was certain had mere hours ago started out as perfectly blow-dried hair. Currently it resembled a mop of windswept curls which, although a lifelong bane to their owner, he'd always found adorably sweet and innocently sexy.

'Jye, they don't love each other! The whole thing is a disaster!'

Stephanie was a hopeless romantic, and consequently her emotions and reactions were always more extreme than reasonable, nevertheless Jye was surprised by how passionately she was reacting to the marriage of two of the firm's employees. 'I didn't realise you and this Karrie were such close personal friends.'

'Well, we were. *Are.* Oh, I don't know!' She drew a deep breath, then expelled it in a heavy sigh. 'We only really got to know each other when I wanted someone to draw up some plans for improving the usefulness of my kitchen…'

It took all Jye's determination not to erupt with laughter. The only *useful* improvement Steff could make to her kitchen was to line it with lead and donate it to the Government for nuclear waste storage. Since the mere memory of her most recent attempt at baking a birthday cake for Duncan was enough to have his stomach recoiling in protest, he hastily dragged his mind back to what she was currently saying.

'We found we had a lot in common, and so after work sometimes we'd go out. Nothing special, just the movies or dinner or a walk at the beach, you know. But one night we went back to my place and…well, it came as a shock to discover we were attracted to each other, but one thing led to another and we ended up necking, and—'

'*You what? Stephanie!*' She jumped at his raised voice. He hadn't meant to shout, but… Hell, he wasn't a prude by a long shot, but—

'Don't look at me like that! Necking is perfectly normal. I'm twenty-six years old and in love with him.'

'*Him*? You mean *Carey*—as in C-A-R-E-Y?'

She shot him a weary frown. '*Yes. Brad Carey* from the design office. Anyway, as I was saying…'

Jye was momentarily deaf to all but the sound of every one of his internal organs sagging with profound relief. He'd mixed his Karries with his Careys and for a second there his broad-minded live-and-let-live attitudes had got a bit weak at the knees.

'Oh, Jye…I just feel so confused.'

'Tell me about it,' he muttered dryly; an unfortunate choice of words since Stephanie took them at face value and began regaling him with an in-depth commentary on her feelings for Carey. In a business crisis Steff could be the Rock of Gibraltar, but when it came to a hiccup in her personal life she sagged with more speed than one of her soufflés; at least around him. With Duncan she always managèd to maintain an air of stoic pragmatism in deference to the older man's deeply entrenched 'stiff upper lip' credo.

'I'm not sure if I'm more miserable or mad,' she said softly, absently dragging the large gold locket she wore back and forth across its chain. 'It was such a shock. Godfather just blurted it out to me the moment I stepped off the plane and…and…'

While Steff rarely cried, the fragile tremble of her glossed mouth and her rapid blinking told Jye it was time to jump in and divert her before things started getting damp.

'Honey, I'm sure all this seems totally devastating to you at this minute, but at the risk of sounding unsympathetic and cynical…well, you fall in love more often than I fall into bed.'

'I do not!'

The expression of wounded outrage was one she had down pat. He'd seen her produce it on countless occasions during their youth, in a bid to convince Duncan of her innocence of any pranks in which they'd been caught, but while she might have been able to con the old man, Jye wasn't as gullible. He stared down the blatant lie, until a sheepish smile tugged at her mouth.

'Oh, all right,' she mumbled. 'Amend that accusation to "more often than you fall into *your own bed*" and I'll agree with you. Except this time it's *different*.'

'Uh-huh.'

'I mean it, Jye,' she stated, her face and voice urgent with conviction. 'What I feel for Brad was—*is*,' she corrected, 'really special. He's…well…he's *unique*.'

'Unique, huh? Imagine that,' he said with pseudo-awe. 'Who'd have thought Brad'd have so much in common with *every other guy you've fallen for in the last ten years*?'

'But that's just it! Brad's *not* like the guys I've fallen for before.' A dreamy smile crept over her face. 'He's intelligent, thoughtful, compassionate, funny and…and…' She waved her arms in an all-encompassing fashion. 'And *everything wonderful*!'

'And *married*!' he reminded her. 'A word that not only

*rings* bells, but even to me conjures up images of rings *and* bells.' An expression of absolute desolation consumed her face, making Jye wish he'd not been quite so brutally smug. Hell, this Carey guy must have really done a number on her! Feeling a royal jerk, he skirted his desk and placed a consoling arm around her dejected shoulders.

'I'm sorry, honey. That wasn't fair. The last thing you need is me rubbing it in. But you can do a whole lot better than a guy who's stupid enough to let you go. *He's* the loser here.'

'Thanks, Jye. But unfortunately that doesn't make me feel any better this time.'

He assumed a comically shocked expression. 'It worked when you busted up with Tom. And with Dick and Harry. Not to mention Happy, Grumpy, Sleepy, Doc and all their predecessors.'

Steff's response to his attempt at humour was nearer a flinch than a smile. 'Yeah, well, I guess after a thousand or so deliveries everything loses impact.'

'Okay, but that doesn't make it any less true. So, how about you stop playing the victim and start looking on the bright side, huh?'

'God, Jye, your sympathy and compassion are just overwhelming me,' she pouted.

'The way I see it, Steff, you're feeling more than sorry enough for yourself as it is. My feeding your misery with false sympathy will only encourage you to mope over the jerk longer.' He tugged on a platinum curl. 'And I happen to think you're a lot more fun when you're ready to take on the world, Stephanie Worthington.' Grinning, he gave her a quick squeeze and kissed the top of her head.

Her hair's silky softness was familiar, but the faint fragrance of her shampoo wasn't. Instinctively he focused on the scent, but was distracted by the way her fingers were fidgeting with the cuff of his shirt and tickling his wrist.

'Jye…'

'Mmm.' *What was that perfume? It wasn't her usual. It was muskier, more earthy.*

'*Jye!*' Her hand was no longer gentle as she tugged at his wrist. 'Are you listening to me?'

'Huh? Eh, sorry, what did you say?'

'I said, you're right...'

'Can I have that in writing?'

Poking out her tongue, she punched his shoulder. 'I'd already decided moping *isn't* going to do my situation any good, which is why I'm here. I need your help, Jye.'

'*My* help?'

She nodded. 'Uh-huh, because this time I'm not going to crawl away like some pathetic, rejected creature and waste months licking my wounds in self-imposed social exile!'

The notion that she'd ever spent even *one week* in self-imposed social exile, much less months, was fanciful in the extreme. For the last ten years of her life Stephanie had flitted from one 'love of her life' to the next, with barely a day or two's recovery time.

'Fighting back, eh? Well, that's a good sign. Let me guess,' he said. 'You're planning to pull the rug out from Mr Opportunistic Carey by telling Duncan his marriage is only a sham to get himself promoted in—'

'Don't be ridiculous!' she exclaimed, looking aghast. 'Godfather would sack him on the spot if he knew.'

'So? What better way to get back at him?'

'But I don't want to get back *at* him, Jye; I just want to *get him* back.'

For a moment Jye thought he'd misheard her, but her satisfied smile told him he hadn't. '*Are you crazy*? The guy is *married*.'

She shook her head. 'Not really. It's not a genuine marriage. They weren't married in a church and they don't sleep together.'

'Carey told you this?' Her expression alone made it a rhetorical question. 'And you *believe* him?'

'Of course. Brad wouldn't lie to me.'

'*Right*. Has it occurred to you that honest old Brad might be trying to have his cake and eat it too?'

'No, it hasn't!' she told him. 'You don't know Brad like I do.'

'I know *you*, Steff, and you sure aren't cut out for the role of mistress! For God's sake, you've always equated infidelity with murder; "emotional rape", you called it, when I dated two girls at once. *And I wasn't sleeping with either one!* Do you really think you're capable of having an affair with a married man and being able to live with yourself?'

'I keep telling you, Jye, he's not *really* married.'

'Listen, he mightn't have gone the route of a high nuptial mass, complete with white lace, bridesmaids and the thousands of guests you and your friends intrinsically associate with being *really* married,' he said snidely. 'But, kiddo, *married is married*! Trust me, his wife isn't going to take kindly to you making a takeover bid on her hubby!

'Regardless of whatever calculating reasons Carey had for marrying the poor woman, I'll bet you dollars to donuts the only reason *she* married him is because she imagines herself in love with him.'

'Oh, Jye, you're so naive!'

The absurdity of the accusation robbed him of speech, but unfortunately Stephanie suffered no such problem.

'It was Karrie Dent who suggested the whole fake marriage idea to Brad in the first place,' she explained. 'Karrie assumed he'd be going for the position of department senior when it became vacant and asked him to recommend she move up into his job. When he told her he wouldn't even be considered for promotion because Godfather liked his senior management married, Karrie came up with the idea of a marriage of convenience.

'You were right with your assessment of her, Jye,' she continued matter-of-factly. 'Karrie is a hardcore career woman through and through. Her interest in Brad is professional, nothing more.'

'Bull!' he countered. 'She might have designs on her professional future, but she's got designs on Carey too. Think about it, Steff. If she was solely after the promotion to his job, she only had to plant the idea of him marrying *someone*…' He paused to lend impact to his words. 'According to what you've said, *she* volunteered herself for the job.'

Doubt clouded Stephanie's wide eyes as she chewed thoughtfully on her lower lip. How was it women could do that? In his vast experience the only downside to kissing a woman was lipstick.

'You're wrong, Jye!' The emphatic declaration refocused his distracted thoughts. 'Karrie told Brad she had no objections to him having outside liaisons during their pseudo-marriage, providing he was discreet.'

Jye groaned. 'Brad told you this too, of course?'

'Yes. And I believe him.'

'Then it's a toss-up whether to nominate you for this year's Miss Gullibility award, or him for an Oscar.'

'*Stop it, Jye,*' she implored. 'Can't you see that what he and Karrie have is just a…a *business arrangement*? A *temporary* business arrangement. What I feel for him is…' She squared her shoulders. 'Well, I truly think I'm in love with him.'

'Well, your thinking stinks!' he roared, no longer able to withhold his frustration. 'My God, Stephanie, can you *hear* yourself? You're standing there trying to justify jumping into a sordid affair with a married man? Well, sunshine, if you're waiting for me to give you my blessing you're going to have a bloody long wait! I mightn't have any time for marriage on a personal level, but I do consider other people's sacred!'

'Oh, stop being so sanctimonious, Jye! I keep telling you it's not a *real* marriage!'

'If it's legal—it's real!'

'It's not *spiritually* real!'

'Give me strength.' Jye looked heavenward for a clue to how to deal with a woman determined to sabotage his sanity. The idea of activating the sprinkler system in the hope a drenching would cool off her overheated hormones was a tempting one. So was strangling her. Somehow, though, he kept both urges at bay.

'Okay,' he said finally, deciding to try another tack. 'Okay, let's pretend that because of your narrow-minded conceptions of what stipulates a *real* marriage Brad Carey is "technically" still unattached. Why, then—I repeat, *why*—are you making such a fuss about it? I mean, given you want him, and he wants you, if you don't consider him "*really married*", what the hell is your problem?'

'The *problem* is,' she retorted, 'everyone knows Karrie doesn't date much, and Brad is so *nice* he feels it isn't right to put her in a position where, if anyone found out he and I were seeing each other, it'd make her look like a fool.'

'The guy's a regular prince!'

Stephanie ignored his sarcasm. 'But to me it doesn't make sense to wait around hoping Karrie will start seeing someone. Good Lord, Jye, all she does is *work*! She's so damned consumed with her career that the only men she's likely to meet are other executives who, thanks to Godfather's medieval thinking, are all married!'

'Well, maybe you'll get lucky and the guy who services the photocopiers will take a fancy to her,' he suggested dryly.

The blonde head shook, as if he'd made a serious suggestion. 'Wishful thinking,' she returned ruefully. 'Scott's gay. I know, because I wasted the best part of a month giving him the come-on last year.'

'*You hit on the copier mechanic?*'

She shrugged. 'The guy's a hunk. Sheesh! Talk about God having a warped sense of humour…'

Before Jye had a chance to digest *that* fascinating aside, she was speaking again.

'Look, Jye, I know you're not exactly comfortable with the idea of me seeing Brad—'

'What was your first clue?'

'*Jye, please!* I need your help. Can't you at least *listen* to me?' Huge blue-grey eyes silently pleaded with him until he felt as if *he* was in the wrong on the issue.

Damn it! *How did she do that?* he wondered, before resigning himself to the fact that he'd doubtless be long dead before he was immune to it. And, as much as he wished he could boot her out of his office and forget they'd ever had this bizarre conversation, he couldn't, not when she was looking so damned vulnerable; Steff and Duncan were the closest thing to family he was ever going have. If he couldn't sympathise with her at the very least he owed it to her to let her talk the problem out of her system.

'Okay,' he said wearily. 'I'm listening. But I'm due in a meeting with Duncan and the finance boys in ten minutes, so you've got eight to say whatever it is you want to say. And *don't*,' he said loudly, when she opened her mouth to speak, 'even *think* of asking me to help you cover your butt if the old man finds out you're sleeping with a married man!'

'I'm not sleeping with him!'

'*You're not?*'

'I've only dated him about a half-dozen times!'

'Bloody hell! Stephanie, you all but told me—'

'My God, Jye,' she gasped, her expression a combination of shock and hurt. 'How could you say such a thing? How could you even *think* I'd just jump into bed with a guy I barely know? How co—'

Jye thumped the desk to cut off her insinuation that *he* was the villain in all this. '*Maybe,*' he said, speaking into the ensuing silence through tightly clenched teeth, 'it's because you've just finished telling me your immediate goal in life is to be the guy's mistress!'

'I never said that!' she denied hotly, no longer looking the slightest bit vulnerable.

'Well, that's the impression I got!'

'*You would!* But, for your information, there's more to love than *sex*. Contrary to *your* personal experience, not *all* relationships between a male and a female are physical.'

'No, not *all*,' he agreed. '*Some are just plain exasperating!*' He met her indignant stare, unsure whether the predominating emotion raging through him was anger or relief.

He *was* relieved by her admission that she and Carey hadn't been lovers, but damn it, he wanted to choke her for letting him think the worst. And more specifically for her stubborn reluctance to write off the relationship.

He studied her, wondering how a woman as attractive, intelligent and educated as Stephanie could be so stupid when it came to her personal life. For all that the sight of her tussled blonde hair, pert little mouth and *too* short skirts at meetings made male clients suspect she was little more than window dressing, Stephanie was a valuable asset to the Porter Resort Corporation. Even if her lifelong goal was marriage, a white picket fence in the suburbs complete with a production line of kids and a Labrador, during business hours she was usually totally focused on her job. If her overtime didn't match that of most of the executive staff it was only because she used her time more efficiently. *Much more efficiently* if she'd also managed to make time with Carey *and* the photocopier mechanic!

'Well?' she demanded, her arms folded like an expectant headmistress greeting a recalcitrant pupil.

'Well, what?'

'I'm waiting for you to apologise for jumping to conclusions.'

Despite himself, Jye felt a smile tug at his mouth at her righteous tone. He fought against it, stubbornly determined not to let her know how easily she could get the upper hand with him. Eventually, though, it was genuine guilt for his words that made him break their duel of silence.

'I didn't so much *jump* to conclusions as get pushed,' he said, holding up a hand when she would have debated the point. 'However, I am sorry for saying what I did.'

Immediate elation shone on her face. 'Then you'll help me?'

He frowned. 'Help you how?'

'By hitting on Karrie for me.'

'*What?*'

'Oh, Jye, *please*?' she begged. 'If you can get Karrie to

go out with *you*, then Brad won't feel guilty about going out with me!'

Rendered speechless by the audacity of her appeal, it was all Jye could do to shake his head, but Stephanie overpowered him even in this small achievement by reaching up to take his face in her palms.

'Don't you see, Jye?' Her voice was light and gentle, no doubt in deference to his still stupefied state. 'It's the perfect solution. In fact it's the *only* solution. And it'll be easy. Karrie won't be able to resist you!

'After all, you're intelligent, rich, handsome, sexy...' She almost purred the word. 'And, better yet, *next in line to take over as head of Porter Resort Corporation*. Face it,' she said, a smug, assured smile slinking across her features. 'As a dedicated career girl, even if Karrie thinks you're the biggest jerk of all time, *not* going out with you would be the worst professional move she could ever make!'

There was some measure of satisfaction in seeing her thick-lashed eyes widen in surprise when his hands quickly closed over her wrists and he pushed her arms wide. Leaning forward and negating the foot or so height advantage he held over her, he rested his nose against hers. *'No.'*

She blinked. 'N-n-no, what?'

*'No*, I'm not going to fall for a sweetheart smile, a soft voice or any of the other feminine wiles you just tried to beat me over the head with. And, *no*, I'm not going to ask Karrie Carey out.'

Her attempt to jerk her arms free brought her upper body up against his; her fury was as evident in the heaving rise of her breasts against his chest as it was in her flushed face. 'She...calls...herself,' she enunciated, 'Karrie *Dent*.'

'She can call herself anything she damned well likes; it doesn't alter the fact she's *married* to Brad Carey.'

His taunting resulted in her making a second, more violent bid for freedom, which he denied her for the space of a heartbeat, tempted to shake some sense into her. But when that benign urge was suddenly overwhelmed by a more disturbing one—the urge to kiss her senseless—Jye hurriedly let her go; then immediately tried to revoke the action when he realised Steff was employing her full body weight to break free. His efforts were in vain, and a nano-second later Stephanie's rear hit the carpet.

Neither of the four-letter words they simultaneously uttered was *ouch!*

Jye was immediately crouching beside her. 'Hell, Steff, are you okay?'

One eyebrow arched drolly in a face that wasn't smiling. 'You mean aside from having a busted tailbone?'

'Honey, I'm sorry,' he said, reaching to aid her to her feet. 'I wasn't expecting—'

'How sorry?' Her eyes glittered with almost childish delight and expectation.

'Not *that* sorry—'

She slapped his hand away. 'Which proves talk's cheap,' she grumbled. 'If you were truly sorry you'd agree to ask Karrie out. It's the least you could do for tossing me onto the floor and bruising my butt.'

Jye gritted his teeth. 'I *did not* toss you onto the floor. And if I thought it'd do any good and knock some sense into your foolish, romantic head I'd paddle your precious butt.'

'And *if I thought it'd do any good*,' she parroted hotly, scrambling to her feet with a haste that provided him with a tantalising display of leg, 'I'd appeal to your kind heart and ask you to reconsider. But obviously you don't have a heart, Jye Fox!'

'Yeah? Well, another thing I don't have is time to stand around while you take a second shot at trying to twist me around your little finger.' Feeling more angry than the situation warranted, he scooped up an armful of folders from his desk. 'See ya, sunshine; I've got a meeting to get to.'

'Jye, wait!' She clutched at his arm. Her face was a worryingly engaging mixture of appeal and calculation. 'What if I promised to cook you a week's worth of meals if you just asked Karrie to one teeny little lunch?'

'Pass. We both know you're a potential emergency ward patient every time you so much as walk into a kitchen; so is anyone who eats your cooking.'

'What if I told you I'd started taking cooking lessons two nights a week?'

The announcement surprised him, but in the wake of the latest little bomb she'd dropped on him only mildly so. She'd always said that when she found her Mr Right she'd stop trying to teach herself to cook through the trial and error method and start taking classes. But, despite whatever misguided notions were spinning about in *her* head, married or not, Carey *wasn't* her Mr Right.

'I'd say,' he responded, clenching his fists to contain his again spiralling frustration, 'that if that's supposed to sway me…it *doesn't*. Right now the only lesson you need to learn, Stephanie, is not to muck around with married men. A hotplate isn't the only thing that'll burn your fingers!'

'Jye, *please*.'

'Sorry, Steff, no go. If you want to screw up your life, then fine; that's up to you! But don't expect me to help you do it.'

Feeling more churned up than at any other time he could remember, Jye left her standing in his office, knowing he only had two choices as to how to deal with the matter. He could either stop by the design department on the way to his meeting and punch Brad Carey's lights out for messing Steff around, or he could behave in a rational manner and stay right out of it until Steff came to her senses her-self…and *then* punch Carey's lights out for messing her around!

# CHAPTER TWO

THE grilled cheese sandwiches were only black on one side, yet not even success in the kitchen was enough to perk up Stephanie's mood. Sighing despondently, she picked up the plate of artistically arranged sandwiches and two napkins and carried them into the living room to join her friend Ellee, who'd refused to let her cancel their regular '*Melrose* night'.

Firm friends since their days at an exclusive convent high school, they'd both studied Hotel Management at college and commenced work with the Porter Resort Corporation within weeks of graduating. Ellee was now an assistant manager in the Sydney hotel, while Stephanie worked in administration, heading the company's promotional department. The fact she was Duncan Porter's goddaughter meant people tended to overlook the fact that Stephanie was qualified for her position as a junior executive with the corporation, but she'd long since given up letting accusations of nepotism get to her. She was good at her job, and if other people didn't perceive her to be sufficiently dedicated to, or grateful for the prestigious position she held, that was their mistake. Just because she viewed her current career as temporary, aspiring to the long-term roles of wife and mother, it didn't mean she didn't like her job; it was just she craved a very different future.

One that once again she'd thought was within her grasp, only to be left with cold, empty hands, she thought despondently.

It didn't take a psychologist to work out that her hunger to be part of a tight family unit stemmed from the loss of her parents at the age of six, and while she loved Duncan Porter dearly, and would always be grateful he'd taken her in and treated her as if she was his daughter, he wasn't

20

really family. Nor was Jye, for all that he and she had grown up as practically brother and sister. For which, she reminded herself, she was extremely grateful! *Who'd want to be genetically connected to a narrow-minded, selfish, sanctimonious jerk like him?*

'I love the sofa, Steff. You have a real knack for decorating.'

Setting the plate of sandwiches onto the coffee table next to the wine cooler, Stephanie managed a small smile for her friend as she lowered herself into the vacant corner of the yellow and white daisy print sofa in question. She'd bought it yesterday, in a bid to cheer herself up, but the reality was the idea had been nothing more than an expensive exercise in futility; her spirits were still lower than a snake's belly. *Although that elevated them considerably above her opinion of one Jye Fox!*

'The cooking classes must be working,' Ellee commented, using a napkin-covered finger to nudge the miniature cheese-centred triangles around the plate. 'Most of these are only burnt on one side.'

'I experimented with a combination of Gruyere and Edam. Let me know what they're like,' she said, reaching for her wine glass.

Her friend frowned. 'Aren't you having any?'

'I couldn't. I'm too depressed to eat.'

'Depressed? Earlier you said you wanted to cancel out because you were too angry and wired to watch TV.'

'I was. Now I'm depressed.'

'Because Jye wouldn't help you out with Brad?'

'No!' she snapped. 'I'm *furious* over that!'

'Well, geez, you don't have to bite my head off…'

Sighing, she slumped back against the sofa. 'Sorry, Elle, didn't mean to jump all over you. It's just I haven't been able to get in contact with Brad since the day before yesterday; he's not due back in the office for almost two weeks.'

'Ah, the honeymoon.'

'*Ellee*! Brad and Karrie *aren't* together! They just took

their vacations at the same time for appearances' sake. You don't have honeymoons after a marriage of convenience.'

'How come?'

'Because there'd be nothing to do, of course!'

Ellee flicked back her long auburn hair and cast a superior look at her friend. 'Holy cow, Steff, you're not that dumb. There's nothing to say sex can't be convenient too.' She grinned. 'Actually, I think the idea of having a good-looking guy under contract, on-site and supposedly off-limits is a bit of a turn-on in itself!'

'You're as bad as Jye! Why can't anybody accept that Brad and Karrie aren't interested in a physical relationship?'

'*Because…*' her friend's tone was one usually reserved for simpletons '…Brad Carey is drop-dead gorgeous and Karrie could moonlight as a model if she was ever pressed for cash.'

'As usual, you're exaggerating, Elle. There are plenty of guys better looking than Brad. And Karrie Dent is too over-endowed to be a model.'

'What you mean is unlike you *she* has a bust.'

'I've got a bust.' Stephanie defended herself with as much conviction as she could muster. 'It's just subtly understated, that's all. Besides, not *all* men are obsessed with boobs and sultry looks, you know. Some, like Brad, prefer intelligence and personality in a woman.'

'Yeah, but not necessarily in bed.'

Stephanie's response to that was silence, dished up with a hard stare.

'Okay, okay. I'm sorry,' her friend said. 'I'm sure everything Brad told you about this marriage of his is true. *Beyond the realms of credibility*,' she inserted drolly. 'But nevertheless true. I have to admit that on the few occasions I've met him, he's always struck me as an up-front, dependable kind of guy.'

Stephanie nodded. *Unlike some men she could name*, that was exactly what Brad was: *dependable*. Although she couldn't help wishing she'd heard about his marriage from him, *prior* to the event, rather than second-hand when it was already a *fait accompli*.

Though she'd only returned to Sydney a few days ago, after five weeks interstate, she and Brad had spoken several times during that period, and while all the calls had started out as business related, *none*, had ended that way. There was no way she'd imagined Brad's interest, but, since the law in New South Wales required a four-week 'cooling off' period between applying for a licence and getting married, Brad had therefore 'technically' been engaged during all their conversations and chosen not to mention it to her.

It hadn't been easy to conceal her shock when her god-father had casually mentioned Brad's promotion to her over dinner three nights ago, after he'd met her at the airport. In the space of a mere heartbeat she'd gone from shocked, disbelieving and heartbroken to flat-out furious!

Never had she been so enraged in her whole life! Not even when she'd been seventeen and Jye, who was only four years older, had ratted to their godfather that Stephanie was dating a twenty-five-year-old. What had really steamed her up at the time was that while Jye was playing moral vigilante over her perfectly innocent romance he'd been in the midst of an affair with a divorcee twice his age! Two-faced as *that* was, it kind of faded into insignificance compared to discovering a guy you were ninety-nine point nine per cent in love with had gone and married someone else.

Somehow she'd managed to maintain a semblance of normality through the meal with Duncan, but the minute she'd got home she was punching Brad's number into the phone while simultaneously patting herself on the back for not having been stupid enough to think he warranted auto dialling. When she'd been unable to contact him, either at his apartment or on his mobile, she'd phoned Jye, hoping for a sympathetic ear, only to have some breathless female answer his phone. Again her emotions had been jerked from despair to anger. Too wound up to sleep, she'd spent the rest of the night alternating between crying and plotting heinous ways of murdering both Brad *and* faceless panting females, then disposing of their body parts in various cages at the zoo.

At work the next day she'd learned from the department secretary that Brad was 'on vacation' and could only be reached in an emergency. Fortunately, one of the advantages of being the goddaughter of the company's owner was being able to say, *'I'd hardly be trying to reach him if it wasn't an emergency, would I?'* and not getting called on it.

There was no doubt Brad had been stunned to hear her voice when she'd finally made contact with him, but she supposed part of that could be excused, since her mode of greeting had been, *"Hello, you miserable, two-faced lump of pond scum."* Or words to that effect. In the end, though, he'd sounded genuinely contrite for not telling her what was going on, explaining that he hadn't wanted her to feel he was putting her in a position where she'd have to choose between loyalty to her godfather and his company over her friendship with him. *That* was the Brad she knew, the one she'd fallen in love with, and as he'd promised, there had been a handwritten letter from him waiting amongst the bundle of mail she'd collected from her neighbour that afternoon.

It was after the one millionth reading of the letter, and the shedding of a corresponding number of tears, that Stephanie had got the idea of finding a distraction for Karrie; with Jye's help, Brad's business-motivated marriage didn't automatically have to mean the death of her budding relationship with him. *But Jye had turned down her appeal for help.*

'Cold-hearted selfish pig that he is!'

*'Excuse me?'* Ellee arched a disbelieving eyebrow. 'I thought Brad was the kindest, most wonderful man God ever created.'

'He is. Jye's the jerk!'

'Jye's a babe.'

'Good looks and sex appeal are not the be all and end all of everything, Ellee.'

'No, Jye Fox is!' she retorted salaciously. 'I'll never forgive you for not fixing me up with him.'

Stephanie didn't bother to stifle her groan. 'Look, Ellee, *I tried*, okay? For you, for Jill, for Kaitlin, for every damn female I ever made the mistake of introducing to him!' She shook her head and leaned forward to refill her wine glass. 'Honestly, sometimes I think the only reason I made so many friends growing up was because I lived in the same house as him.'

'Steff…'

'Mmm?'

*'It was.'*

Her friend's deadpan expression succeeded in making Stephanie laugh.

'Well, that's something at least!' Ellee said with approval. 'Is it me or this rapidly dwindling bottle of wine that's improving your mood?'

'Both.' She winked. 'Plus the fact I'm expecting Brad to phone tonight. Pass me a sandwich, will you?'

Ellee frowned. 'You sure? I've picked out all the edible ones.

'*All* of them! I thought you were on a diet.'

'Steff… I only ate two.'

'Oh. Well, what's the verdict?'

'Let me put it this way…*don't skip any more cooking lessons.*'


The call from Brad hadn't come by the time Ellee left a little after ten p.m. It hadn't come by midnight, when a dejected Stephanie finally took herself off to bed, nor by three-fifteen a.m., when she was lying awake, cradling the portable phone. And it still hadn't come when she sat at her desk alone in her office at a little after eight the next morning.

'Stephanie!'

She jumped at the unexpected appearance of her godfather.

'I was hoping you'd be in early!' he said, his pleasure at finding this the case evident in his beaming smile.

'Oh? Why's that?' she asked, forcing her mind into business mode. Despite the close personal relationship she and Jye shared with the tall, elderly man, Duncan's own rigid discipline in not allowing it to surface in the office had conditioned them to do the same.

'Because I need you packed and out at the airport in time to make an eleven o'clock flight.'

'Aw, Duncan,' she groaned. 'Don't do this to me. I've just got back from five weeks interstate. Can't you send someone else?'

'I already have. Jye left two days ago.'

*He had?* Well, damn! And here she'd been, thinking how effectively she'd been avoiding him.

'Apparently he's got a problem—'

*'More than one if you ask me.'*

Her godfather frowned. 'He's discussed the planned purchase of Illusions with you? Well, good! It'll save me doing it.'

Stephanie shook her head. 'No. No, I haven't discussed anything with him since I got back.' At least not business, and not successfully, she silently amended. 'I didn't even know he was away.'

'He's over negotiating the purchase of Sir Frank Mulligan's Illusion Island complex. I think it'll be a valuable addition to our group, but he's hit a snag.'

Stephanie hoped he'd hit it *really* hard—with his head! 'What kind of snag?' she asked.

Duncan Porter's left hand waved the question aside. 'We had a poor mobile connection, so discussing it would've been impossible. Besides, I don't need the added stress of the negotiations involved in this side of things. Jye's head of Expansion and Development; whatever the problem is he'll handle it. I trust his judgement completely.'

'Then why do you want me to fly out there?'

'Because Jye says it's crucial to us securing the deal.'

'I don't see how it could be. My role in the scheme of

things is a long way down the track from property acquisition. What could Sir Frank want to discuss with Porter's
promotions executive?'

Her godfather's bushy grey eyebrows drew to a sharp
'V', making the soft, unexpected jowls in his otherwise
long, angular face appear more pronounced. Standing six
feet tall, tanned and reed-thin, with white hair that needed
both cutting and conditioning, even in his impeccably tai-
lored suit he reminded Stephanie of a hardened old sea
captain.

'It's common knowledge Mulligan's something of an eccentric, so who knows what hoops he might want us to
jump through to secure the sale?' he said. 'Perhaps he
merely wants to be assured that we're committed to main-
taining the Illusions Hotel as one of the finest in the country.'

Stephanie sent him a sceptical look. 'Duncan, he's only
got to look at our track record to know that. Besides, he's
spent a veritable fortune competing against us for years.'

Again she earned his trademark dismissive wave. 'Look,
I'm only speculating as to why Jye says he needs you, but
as far as I'm concerned if he thinks it's vital for you to be
brought in on these negotiations, that's good enough for
me.'

While Stephanie usually considered the absolute faith
Duncan showed in all his executive staff admirable, she was
eager to undermine it on this occasion. No way was she in
any frame of mind to personally bail Jye Fox out of a difficult situation!

'That's all well and good, Duncan,' she conceded. 'But
unfortunately at the moment the best I can do is agree to
send Lewis, my assistant. I've been away from my desk for
over a month, and I've got weeks of work here that—'

'That can wait,' her godfather insisted. 'I appreciate your
diligence, Stephanie, but this deal is important to me. I
don't want to see Mulligan sell to someone else and find
myself competing with an unknown quantity or, God for-
bid, that crook Kingston!'

Cole Kingston was a self-made millionaire who'd made his fortune buying up semi-successful Australian resorts and selling them to foreign interest. While not against the law, this automatically made him a crook and arch rival to Duncan, who was a strong believer in keeping Australian businesses in Australian hands.

'Now, Stephanie. I want you to delegate whatever you feel can't wait until you get back and then get on home and pack.'

'I haven't *unpacked* since I got back from Western Australia,' she muttered.

'Good, good. In that case perhaps I can get your tickets changed to an earlier flight,' he murmured, checking his watch before his clear blue eyes came to rest intently on Stephanie. 'You don't look like you're getting nearly enough sleep,' he observed. 'There are circles under your eyes.'

Gosh, *there* was a surprise! 'Things have been a little…eh, hectic since I got back, Duncan,' she hedged. She didn't want him worrying, but nor was she about to get into the details of Brad's sham marriage either.

'You're far too work-orientated for your own good, Stephanie. Why don't you take a few days off once the deal with Mulligan is clinched to relax? In fact why not stay on there?' he suggested. 'Illusion Island really is a wonderful, stress-free spot to relax.'

Yeah, right. Illusion Island was a thirty-minute helicopter flight from mainland Queensland and devoid of telephones, which meant there'd be no way for Brad to contact her and no way for her to avoid Jye! *Wonderful? Stress-free?* In her dreams!

'This had better be good Jye Fox!' she told him as he met her at Cairns airport.

'Hug me!' he demanded, blocking her path to the luggage carousel.

'Do wha—?' Her stunned words were choked off as he hauled her against him.

'Put your arms around my neck.'

'I'd like to put a noose around—*Jye!*'

Shock didn't come close to describing the stunned sensation that assailed her at finding herself enveloped in a fierce bear hug with her head held firmly against a muscular chest. And her attempt to pull away was defeated by sheer masculine strength.

'Act as if you've missed me like crazy,' she was urged by a rough whisper that grazed her ear. 'We're being watched.'

'In your case no doubt by the men in white coats!' she muttered, trying to wriggle free. 'Jye, let go! *Are you nuts?*'

'Damn it, Steff,' he hissed, nuzzling her neck. 'Go with me on this. Act like you missed me. Put some conviction behind it!'

'The only thing I'm going put conviction behind is my knee, when I aim it at your groin! Now...' The hand at the back of her neck angled her head, allowing her to at least be able to confront his face instead of trying to talk through the fabric of his shirt and the wall of his chest. *'Would you mind telling me—?'* Stephanie didn't even have time to gasp as her words were cut off by his mouth.

While it was hardly flattering to Jye's male ego to have a woman stiffen to the consistency of petrified wood in his arms, he consoled himself with the knowledge that it was only Stephanie, and that at least she'd stopped wriggling against him. Now all he had to hope was she'd be too stunned by his behaviour to haul back and smack him in the chops the minute he let her go, because that would blow his story sky-high and any chance of securing the deal with Mulligan along with it.

And he was going to let her go...any second now.

He was only prolonging the moment because he knew Frank and Tory Mulligan, *especially Tory*, would be watching them. The immediate future of the Porter Resort Corporation was hanging on this kiss...it was his responsibility to make it look convincing. He was performing entirely for his audience's benefit, not his own, he reminded

himself as his lips savoured the surprisingly pleasant fla-
vour of Steff's lipstick.

His selfless dedication to the best interests of the company was finally negated by a persistent pressure against
his shoulders, and he slowly lifted his head and opened his
eyes to find a pair of shellshocked blue-grey ones gazing
dazedly up at him. Actually, right now they were more *grey*
than blue, which startled him; never once had he seen
Steff's eyes take on that depth of colour before.

'Jye...' She stopped to draw in a long breath. Jye did
likewise, irritated to find the stress of getting through the
next few minutes was disrupting his breathing; usually he
thrived on pressure. Anxiously he glanced over his shoulder
and discovered Frank Mulligan and his curvaceous third
wife were rapidly approaching them.

'Steff,' he said quickly, cupping her beautiful, bemused
face, 'I need you to go along with everything I'm about to
say. The future of the company is riding on it.'

Sensing a refusal in the way her eyebrows started to
climb, Jye snatched her slender left hand into his much
larger right and swung around to smile broadly at the
Mulligans.

'Sir Frank, Lady Mulligan,' he said, drawing Steff closer
to his side. 'I'd like you to meet my wife...'

# CHAPTER THREE

'YOUR wife! *Your wife!*' Stephanie exploded in a furious whisper, the moment the Mulligans were temporarily out of earshot. 'I'd sooner be introduced as a nymphomaniacal axe murderer! At least *that* would leave me with some dignity and credibility!'

'Cut the theatrics, Steff,' Jye told her, his gaze drifting across to where the Mulligans were now speaking with a prominent politician awaiting a departing flight. 'They'll be back in a few minutes and we've got to get our story straight.'

'*Our* story! This is your tale of horror! I can't think of one reason why I shouldn't just expose it for the crock of—'

'*Because,*' Jye's tone was no less sharp for its low pitch, 'Duncan desperately wants this deal to go through and he's counting on me to deliver it.'

'Well, I know from recent personal experience people don't always get what they want; *especially not if they're counting on you!*'

Stephanie felt a tingle of victory as her barbed remark tightened his mouth.

'Look, this isn't anything like what you wanted me to do.'

'You've got that right! All *I* wanted was for you to ask a poor lonely woman out and make *three* people happy. *You* want me to expose myself to public ridicule and pretend I'm married to you!'

'Hey! A lot of women happen to think I qualify as a terrific catch.'

'A lot of women think of prostitution as a valuable public service too, but I'm not civic-minded enough to make it *my* career choice!'

'Just as well,' he mumbled. 'If that kiss was your best effort at faking passion, you'd starve to death.'

The only thing that kept Stephanie from responding to *that* with a very *passionate* kick to his shins was the sight of Sir Frank Mulligan shaking hands with the federal senator he'd been conversing with; in just a matter of moments she'd be expected to resume her role of devoted wife. Thanks to the politician's fortuitous arrival she'd hadn't thus far been required to do more than endure a narrow-eyed appraisal from Lady Mulligan while the woman's much older husband had congratulated Jye on not only having a head for business, but an eye for beauty. At that juncture Mulligan had spied the high-profile politician and hastily excused himself, and his somewhat reluctant wife, to hustle off to speak with the man.

Now the Mulligans' return was imminent, and Stephanie still didn't have a clue as to why Jye had concocted the story he had, except that the Illusion purchase supposedly hinged on it. Farfetched as that seemed, either she had to accept it at face value for the present or risk blowing the deal for Porter Resorts. Much as she'd love to say, *Forget it, Jye, you're on your own!* she couldn't.

'Okay,' she said resignedly. 'What's the story?' The relief in his face would have been laughable had she currently been in the mood to find anything about Jye Fox even remotely amusing.

'We've been married six months,' he said quickly. 'Apart from that we're ourselves; you're just back from five weeks in WA, but you couldn't fly out here with me because of unfinished business. The fewer lies we tell the safer we'll be.'

'And the reason for this charade?'

'Er…long story. There's no time to get into it now. I'll tell you later.'

The evasive way he hastily bent to pick up her luggage sent Stephanie's suspicion meter through the roof. Clutching his upper arm, she squeezed it until coal-black eyes lifted to hers. As she'd suspected, his face reflected the slightly stupid expression males invariably wore whenever they tried to conceal guilt with innocence.

'Tell me *now, darling,*' she said, producing a sugary smile. 'Or this loving reunion is down the toilet.'

'Steff, it's noth—'

*'Tell me.'*

'If you must know,' he hissed, 'Tory Mulligan sees me as an old flame worth reigniting.'

Stephanie rolled her eyes. 'I should've guessed! That explains the poisonous looks she's been throwing at me. Does Sir Frank know?'

'I don't think so, but…' Jye sent another uncomfortable look in the direction of the other couple. 'Mulligan's insanely jealous; unless we can convince them both I'm not the slightest bit interested in flirtatious Tory, he's likely to boot us off the island and say "no dice" to selling to Porter's.'

His mouth tightened to a grim line. 'We're going to have to act our little butts off.'

'You're going to owe me big time for this, Jye Fox.'

'But you'll do it?'

'Don't fret, *darling*, I'll be the best wife you ever had!' She chuckled at his pained expression.

'Don't make the mistake of underestimating them,' he cautioned. 'Mulligan might be an eccentric, but he's a shrewd old devil, and Tory isn't as dumb as she looks.'

'Perhaps,' Stephanie said, slipping her arm through his and smiling up at him for the benefit of the curvaceous brunette and the grey-haired man who were rapidly nearing them. 'But she'd still only need an IQ in the low twenties to qualify as the *brightest* flame you've ever had!'

The trip out to the island was made in the Mulligans' private chopper, with Sir Frank himself at the controls. A poor seat selection on Jye's part had him situated directly behind him, ideally placed to receive Tory's *'I don't consider her competition'* glances from the front passenger seat, and Stephanie's *'just wait till we're alone'* visual threats from alongside him. If looks could kill, Jye figured he was going to die of multiple wounds before they landed.

When Mulligan insisted they all wear headsets with microphones to allow for conversation over the sound of the rotor blades, he started worrying that Tory might begin asking awkward questions about their marriage which would have Steff contradicting what he'd already said. While he had no doubts they could pull this hare-brained charade off once they got a chance to fine-tune things, he cursed whatever female thinking had caused a woman who loved jewellery as much as Steff did, and who usually wore at least three or four rings at a time, to choose today of all days not to wear any!

He could only make sure that he kept Steff's left hand hidden within his as much as possible, and that Tory would be too busy assessing her competition's physical attributes to note the absence of a wedding ring. Fortunately, though, the moment the headsets went on Mulligan began a non-stop monologue of what the island had been like when he'd purchased it twenty-three years ago, and how it had been his vision and financial genius which had turned it into the multi-billion-dollar enterprise it was today.

So far no one had been able to get a word in edgeways, and Jye was momentarily grateful for the fact he'd already heard the story, three times in as many days; if the old guy did falter he could prompt him with, *Sir Frank, tell Steff about how you...* before Tory could open her mouth and do any damage.

They were treated to a low-level aerial view of the island's natural features, and the manmade ones that contributed to the Illusion Resort Complex. Stephanie was suitably complimentary, but not to the extent where Sir Frank would feel confident about raising his already exaggerated asking price for the island. It was a relief to know that no matter how ticked off Steff might be with him, she wouldn't allow her feelings to be detrimental to the negotiations. She might be a hopelessly romantic idealist, whose lateral thinking was beyond all comprehension to him, but she was also the most loyal person Jye knew. No way would she let him or the Porter Resort Corporation down.

'I'm afraid, because Jye didn't tell us you were flying out until this morning, Stephanie, we don't have one of our larger suites available until tomorrow,' Sir Frank told her as he helped her into a motorised golf cart for the trip from the helipad to the hotel. 'However, if you feel Jye's current suite is a little…er, *cramped* for two people—*despite it being one of our most prestigious,*' he hastened to add. 'Then Victoria and I would be delighted to have you both spend the evening with us in our penthouse.' He smiled at his wife. 'Wouldn't we, Peaches?'

The bitch in Stephanie would have liked to attribute 'Peaches's' vacant expression as proof that she *was* as stupid as Stephanie's earlier claims, but in all fairness it was more likely she'd not heard her husband's invitation, being so preoccupied with sending laser-hot glances to Jye behind his back. Behind Sir Frank's back, that was, not Jye's. Jye had taken the full impact of Tory's torrid speculation front-on, and Stephanie figured when he took off his shirt he'd have third-degree burns to prove it. Lady Mulligan was about as subtle as the bowling-ball-size diamond she wore on her left hand.

'Beautiful, isn't it?' the brunette cooed, noting the direction of Stephanie's gaze and thrusting the huge rock into her face. 'Frank selected the stone, but I designed the setting.'

That bit of information immediately had Stephanie upgrading her opinion of Lady Mulligan's intelligence, since such an undertaking would have required at least an honours degree in engineering. There appeared to be as much meshing and interlocking of metal supporting the ostentatious diamond as there was the Sydney Harbour Bridge.

'It's…it's quite unique.' Stephanie said, catching the silent worry in Jye's eyes before his attention was reclaimed by the grey-haired man at his side. 'I've never seen so much detail done in white-gold before.'

'It's platinum, actually. I'm allergic to *cheap* metals,

aren't I, darling?' Tory said, smiling at her husband as he assisted her into the cart.

'Much to the distress of my accountants, who have no idea how much a man wants to please the woman he loves!' He chuckled and winked at Jye. 'I think it would be a good idea to let the girls sit in the back together. That way they can discuss jewellery and fashion to their hearts' content while we talk business.

Stephanie let the sexist remark go unchallenged, noting that Jye wasn't any more thrilled by Sir Frank's idea than she was. There was a message in his eyes as they met hers clearly warning her to stay on her toes, and within moments she understood his concern.

'I gather *you* aren't overly fond of jewellery, Stephanie,' Tory said, the instant they were mobile. 'I couldn't help noticing you don't wear *any* rings.'

Jye's stomach dropped at both the question and its tone. This was what he'd been dreading; the Victorian Inquisition! Mentally willing Steff not to say the wrong thing, he struggled to keep one ear on what Mulligan was saying to him about recent stockmarket movements and the other on the conversation in the back seat.

'Oh, but I *adore* jewellery!' Stephanie responded with a delighted laugh Jye recognised as forced. 'Earrings, bracelets, rings…you name it, I've got dozens. Isn't that right, Jye?' she asked, without giving him a chance to respond. 'Unfortunately I tend to puff up when I fly, so I can't wear anything too tight. See?' As proof her hands were thrust between the front and rear seats, no doubt so Sir Frank could also observe them. Glancing at them, Jye supposed the long, elegant fingers might have been a fraction swollen, but only someone who knew her very well would have noticed, and Tory didn't look entirely convinced.

'Don't worry, they'll be back to normal in a few hours,' Steff continued, as if everyone had gasped with horror. 'And I'll be able to wear my rings again. I have to admit I feel positively *naked* without them.'

'I know what you mean,' Tory agreed. 'There's nothing like a wedding ring to make a person feel *truly* married. Which, of course, is why so many men *refuse* to wear one… Tell me, does Jye wear one?'

Jye noted the pointed pause and barely resisted the urge to say, *Cut the crap, Tory, you know damned well I don't!* He could only assume Steff must have shaken her head, because Tory's next question was a horrified, *'And that doesn't give you cause for concern?'*

'No.' Steff's response was magnificently matter-of-fact. 'Why should it?'

'Oh…well, no reason, really…I suppose,' Tory said, with theatrical hesitation. 'It's just that most women I know would feel *cheated* if their husbands didn't *want* to wear a wedding ring. After all, not only does it advertise that a man is off-limits to other women, but it's the ultimate statement of his absolute commitment to his marriage.'

*'Really? How strange…'*

Jye fought a smile at the incredulous tone Stephanie injected into her response.

*'All* of the women *and* men I know consider the *taking of marriage vows* as the ultimate statement of commitment.'

'Now remember what I said, Stephanie,' Sir Frank said as they entered the plush reception foyer of the resort's main building. 'We'd love to have you as our guests tonight if—'

'Oh, no, Sir Frank! We wouldn't dream of encroaching on your private space. After all, you and Jye *are* involved in business discussions, and I'm a firm believer in keeping business and personal relationships separate.

*Not that Lady Victoria has any such inhibitions!* Stephanie thought, noting the 'lady' in question was again directing her bedroom eyes and sexy pouts in Jye's direction. Terrific! At this rate she was either going to have to cling to Jye like a wetsuit twenty-four hours a day, or follow Tory around with a bucket of cold water!

'Actually, Sir Frank,' she said, offering her best smile,

'I'm intrigued by those cottages we flew over at the other end of the island. I don't suppose there'd be any chance Jye and I might be able to stay in one of those?'

'*A cottage?*' Jye looked even more surprised by the request than Sir Frank. Stephanie sent him what she hoped would pass as a 'cajoling wife' smile.

'Oh, darling, I know how you hate not being able to get immediate room service,' she said. 'But after spending the last five weeks with Porter housemaids and bellboys fawning over me I really would like to relax in a little less commercial atmosphere. The *isolation* and *solitude* of a cabin away from the main resort seems like heaven. And, well…we haven't really had any time *alone* since I returned from Perth.'

Sir Frank's chuckle told her he'd interpreted her words in exactly the way she'd intended, while the flash of approval in Jye's eyes meant he'd grasped her more subtle message to him: the further away they were from the Mulligans the better off they'd be.

'Great idea, sweetheart…' Jye's voice was pitched low and had the consistency of warm honey as he draped an affectionate arm around her shoulder and squeezed her close, smiling down into her face. 'I agree…a cottage would be perfect.'

Wow! Talk about acting potential! Jye was so much the loving husband she got butterflies just meeting his gaze. When he continued watching her as if waiting for a further response, Stephanie wondered if perhaps grateful wives were supposed to kiss their husbands at times like this. Probably, she decided, but chose to err on the side of caution and merely bestowed a beaming smile on him. Given the hangover effect of Jye's earlier kiss at the airport, the less they fooled around with *that*, the better off she'd be.

'What about it, Sir Frank?' Jye said, continuing to hold her against him. 'Is there a cottage available?'

'We'll soon find out. And if there is, I'll ensure room service is extended to you around the clock, rather than just between seven a.m. and ten p.m.'

'That's very generous of you, Sir Frank,' Jye said. 'But completely unnecessary. After five weeks away from my wife, the only *room service* I'll need during the night won't require a call to Reception.'

Stephanie almost choked on the heat that rushed to her face as Sir Frank's hearty male laughter rang through the reception area, drawing every eye to them. Tucked beneath Jye's arm, she felt like an absolute bimbo, but his grip was as deliberate as the smile he fixed on her.

The rat was enjoying this, damn him! For ten cents she'd have shrugged free of his 'affectionate' arm and the phoney caress of his fingers against her neck and stormed out of the resort. For a lot less she'd have socked him in his too handsome, toothpaste-perfect smile. Instead, reminding herself that the most important thing was to secure the purchase of the resort, she slipped her arm around his waist and furtively pinched him. Hard. Really hard. *With her nails!*

Though Jye gave no outward sign she'd caused him any pain, he nevertheless quickly released her to join Sir Frank and a uniformed clerk at the reception desk, leaving Stephanie standing aimlessly in the middle of the lobby and feeling even more conspicuous. Moving towards a cluster of cane armchairs, she encountered the stony expression of Lady Mulligan waiting for the elevator.

Without the audience of her husband, the stunningly attractive brunette made no attempt to conceal her dislike of Stephanie, and the message in her emerald-green eyes would have been clear to any woman over the age of fifteen. *Be warned. I know what I want and I mean to get it.*

Stephanie had no doubt that if Tory had still been single Jye would have snapped up what she was offering in a second, regardless of whether he was on a business trip or not. The woman was exactly his type. Beautiful, tall, well endowed—okay, *very* well endowed, Stephanie amended, knowing it was petty to understate the woman's obvious attributes when she'd gone to all the trouble of forcing them into a skintight designer label to accentuate them. But while there was no doubt Lady Victoria Mulligan knew she had the sexual armoury to go into battle for the attention of Jye Fox, there was one thing she *didn't* know that Stephanie did...despite his playboy reputation and legendary sexual liaisons, Jye *actually considered marriage sacred.*

Astounding as that revelation had seemed to her a couple of days ago, Stephanie knew once Jye made up his mind on something *nothing and nobody* could change it. Tory could stand there looking as determined as Joan of Arc and throwing down silent challenges to Stephanie until her silicone melted, but the fact was no matter how much she wiggled her hips, pouted her lips or jiggled her bits in Jye's direction it wasn't going to do her a damn bit of good!

Stephanie swallowed a giggle as she imagined the possible lengths the woman might go to in a bid to tempt Jye. While she accepted that in a battle of sex appeal against Tory *she'd* be going in virtually unarmed, the bitch in her was unable to resist the malicious fun of watching this *femme fatale* knock herself out in a war of seduction she couldn't possibly win. With the purchase of Illusion Island at stake, Stephanie could have had two heads and the body of a pretzel; Jye wasn't going to risk looking twice at Tory if she stripped naked and sat in his cereal bowl!

But *she* didn't know that. She of the lush curves, pouty mouth and *you-might-have-him-but-I'll-get-him* eyes was already confidently manning her torpedoes.

*Well, I might look like a row boat in your eyes, Lady Mulligan,* Stephanie thought, *but we'll see who gets blown out of the water!*

Feeling decidedly smug, she narrowed her eyes and visually semaphored her response to the curvaceous brunette's obvious challenge—*Go ahead... Hit me with your best shot!*

# CHAPTER FOUR

As Jye had suspected, Stephanie's loving wife routine ended the instant they were alone in their cottage.

'I might've agreed to save your butt and rescue this deal by pretending to be married to you, Jye Fox,' she told him, advancing with a wagging finger. 'But I *do not* appreciate being cast in the role of the doting little woman or referred to as "room service".'

'I never referred to you as room service. What I said was—'

'I *know* what you said! You implied I was so hot for your body you only had to snap your fingers of a night to get anything you wanted.'

'Actually, the implication was *I was hot for you*,' he corrected, grinning. 'And only *after* you'd batted those long lashes of yours and announced you wanted a cottage so you could be alone with me.'

Indignantly she jerked away. 'I'll admit there was a lot lash-batting in your direction, but *I* wasn't the one doing it! You ought to be damned grateful I came up with a way of minimising the amount of time we have to spend with them.'

'Yeah, the cabin idea was a stroke of genius,' he agreed, surveying his surroundings as Stephanie opened one of the two interior doors leading from the room and disappeared from sight. 'Unfortunately—' he raised his voice so she could hear him '—it didn't get us out of having dinner with them tonight.'

The main room of the cabin was slate-floored and divided into dining and living space by the placement of furniture and two woven cotton floor rugs. In one corner three wicker-backed bar chairs were placed near a servery, the space above it sealed by louvred shutters which he pulled back to reveal a kitchenette.

'Not bad,' he murmured, turning as Stephanie re-entered the room through the second door.

'You say that now, but you'll change your tune when you find out there's only one bedroom and *one* bed.'

'We' re supposed to be married. I could hardly ask for *two*, now, could I?'

'I realise that!' she snapped. 'But I thought there'd be a fold-up bed somewhere. All *our* resorts provide fold-up beds.'

'So when Porters take over the place we'll make them available. In the meantime we'll have to make do.'

She gave him a droll look. 'In that case you want to hope the sofa opens into a bed, or you'll be stretching out on the floor.'

'Whaddya mean?'

'I mean, Jye,' she said, as if speaking to a simpleton, 'that one of the two people currently standing in this room *won't* be sleeping on a nice luxurious waterbed. But I will be.'

He frowned at the two-seater sofa Stephanie was busy inspecting and cringed. Always a restless sleeper, Jye knew he'd spend the night belting himself against the arms of it, even if by some miracle it could accommodate his six-foot-five length.

'It'd be more democratic for us to toss for it,' he said.

'Definitely. But since I didn't get a vote on coming here, or even *asked* if I wanted to, I'm not advocating democratic rights for *you*.

'Da-da!' she said, when she finally unfolded the sofa. 'Your matrimonial bed! Of course, dear husband, if you want to sleep on sheets you'll have to make it up yourself, because that's as far as I go without a ring on my finger.'

'Aw, c'mon, Steff. Have a heart. I can't sleep on that; it's too short. My legs will hang off the end.'

'So curl them up.'

'I can't sleep curled up. You know I like to sprawl out when I sleep.'

She laughed. 'Actually, Jye, I'm in that minute percentage of the female population between the ages of eighteen and forty who *don't* have an intimate knowledge of your habits in bed. But I guess I could ask *Lady Mulligan* to verify your story.'

'Very funny,' he muttered. 'Even Duncan knows I'm a restless sleeper.' Moving to the pygmy-length contraption, he lowered himself onto it and groaned. The cast he'd worn after breaking his leg skiing hadn't been this rigid!

'I'll never be able to sleep on this thing!' he complained, but Stephanie looked blissfully unconcerned as she carried her luggage into the bedroom. Deciding he needed a drink, he swung himself to his feet from the hardest bed he'd had outside of a tent and headed for the bar fridge.

'Don't get too comfortable in there,' he called out. 'Because this isn't settled.'

'Yes, it is,' she responded. 'I might be here under sufferance, but I'm not going to suffer while I'm here!'

'Be reasonable, Steff. You can't seriously expect me to successfully negotiate a multi-million-dollar hotel purchase if I'm the victim of sleep deprivation and a bad back?'

His words drew laughter from the other room. 'Oh, puuullleeease! That sofa isn't going to make one iota of difference to your negotiating skills!'

'And what makes you so certain of that?'

'That lack of sleep and a bad back won't dull your business acumen?'

'Yeah,' he called, pulling the tab from a can of Queensland beer.

'Why, your impressive history of triumphs in both bedrooms and boardrooms across the country!' she retorted. 'Call me cynical, but I'm willing to bet this won't be the first deal you've negotiated after too much bed and too little sleep.'

'You're cynical! *And* you'd lose the bet!' he lied, grinning to himself. 'I'm fixing myself a drink; you want one?'

'Yeah, thanks. I won't be long.'

Since gin and tonic and white wine were the extent of Steff's taste for alcohol, and she only drank wine with her meals, Jye didn't need to ask what she wanted. By the time she reappeared he'd taken the drinks out onto the small paved patio shaded by a perfumed tropical vine.

She'd changed from the business suit she'd arrived in to a pair of baggy shorts and an equally baggy T-shirt; not surprisingly she was bare-footed. With artless grace she dropped down onto the sun lounger and reached for her drink.

'Ta,' she said, holding her glass towards him. 'To the successful purchase of Illusion Island.'

'Which sadly depends on an undersprung sofa.'

'Stop whining, Jye. If you'd slept in one less bed, you mightn't be in this position today.'

'Care to explain that cryptic comment?'

'Tory.' She grinned as he groaned. 'Enough said?'

'More than enough. I almost died when I found out she was married to Mulligan. Thank God I hadn't let things get too far. I—'

An alarm bell went off in Stephanie's head. Ricocheting upright, she glared at him. 'Whaddya mean, *thank God you hadn't let things get too far*? Exactly how *far* are we talking about here?'

There was enough consternation on Jye's face to tell her that something had happened between him and his old flame Tory before he'd learned she was Lady Frank Mulligan. She swore.

'Damn it to hell, Jye! You didn't sleep with her, did you?'

'Of course not! Well, not since I've been here anyway.' He withstood her laser-like stare for about five seconds before letting out a resigned sigh.

'Look, the day I arrived here Mulligan had been unexpectedly called to Brisbane on business,' he explained. 'So I figured it was a good opportunity to scout out the island without being fed a whole lot of propaganda designed to nudge up the price...'

When he paused and glanced at her, as if trying to gauge her reaction so far, Stephanie kept her expression impassive. 'Go on,' she said, even though she knew she really didn't want to hear was going to come next. She just *knew* it.

'Well, while I was walking along Mulligan's private beach at the other end of the island I ran into Tory. And naturally, being an old friend, I stopped to speak with her.'

'Oh, *naturally*,' she couldn't resist saying. 'And *naturally* it's too much to expect that she immediately told you how blissfully happy she was married to a grey-haired old lecher with tons of money and a title who just happened to be the owner of the resort?'

Though his face gave him away, Stephanie, for reasons she couldn't explain, pushed for an answer. 'Well? Did the fact she was married to Frank Mulligan come up or not?'

'Not exactly... She just started out talking about old times, and then—'

'And *then*,' she interrupted, 'being as practised as you are in hitting on women, your eagle eyes *immediately* noticed that oversized bowling ball she calls a ring, and you said, "Oh, congratulations, Tory! I see you're married."'

Erring on the side of caution, Jye kept his amusement at her theatrical tone under wraps. 'Um, not exactly... She, er, wasn't wearing any jewellery.'

'I see...and what exactly *was* she wearing?'

'Not a lot.'

'Uh-huh. Tell me, Jye, was she in fact wearing *anything*?'

The appreciative gleam in his eyes and the smirk he was fighting to keep at bay answered her question far more eloquently than words could have, and set her teeth on edge. Why was it that men couldn't embrace the 'less is more' theory? Why was it that a man of Jye's intellect was still attracted to women who practised the "if you've got it flaunt it' ideology and were flat out holding a conversation that required them to supply more than their name and telephone number?

'Don't look so steamed, Steff,' he told her. 'Would it make you feel any better if I said she was wearing a really distracting smile and I never looked lower than her neck?'

It was the patronisingly teasing tone in his voice that snapped the fragile hold she had on her temper. And it was purely an impulsive reaction to toss her drink at him!

Jye's reactions were equally quick as he sprang forward in his chair, pulling his shirt away from his body. *'What the—?'*

'I can't believe you'd humiliate me like that! You hit on her, didn't you?'

'No! She came on to me and—'

'How could you humiliate me like this? How could you talk me into this marriage and not tell me th—'

*'What the hell are you going on about?* We aren't really married!'

*'And thank God for that!'* she spat vehemently. 'You are the most insensitive jerk I've ever met!'

'Aren't you forgetting double-dealing Brad?'

'Leave Brad out of this! He'd never treat me the way you have.'

'Like hell! The guy led you on, then married someone else on the quiet!'

'At least he's never *publicly* humiliated me! My God, no wonder Tory was sending me all those smug looks. She knows you for what you really are—an over-sexed two-timing pig!'

'I told you, nothing happened between us! For heaven's sake, I was wearing a pair of swimming shorts *without pockets*!'

She blinked, caught off guard. 'What does what *you* were wearing have to do with anything?'

'Think about it, Steff. *No pockets.* Do you really think I'm stupid enough to take the risk of unprotected sex with someone I run into on a beach?'

It took her a moment to grasp his point: no pockets, no wallet. *No wallet, no condoms.*

'That's all well and good, Jye,' she said, refusing to acknowledge the wave of relief surging through her. 'But there are lots of ways of being intimate without actually having sex.'

'And no doubt Brad educated you on a few of the finer points.'

The terse remark made her blush, even though she had no reason to feel guilty or embarrassed. 'This has nothing to do with Brad! *He* wasn't the one necking with Tory Mulligan behind her spouse's back!'

'Of course not. *You're* the one he wants behind *his* spouse's back!' Jye retorted, unbuttoning his shirt with rough impatience. 'And I wasn't *necking*, as you so quaintly put it! *She* kissed me.'

Wadding his shirt, he mopped his chest. *'Once.'*

'Yeah, right. And she was just a mass of bruises today from you fighting her off too.'

'I didn't have to *fight her off*! The minute she heard the sound of the resort helicopter she grabbed her beach coat and bolted. End of story.'

'Well, end of *that* particular chapter anyway,' he amended. 'You could've knocked me over with a feather that night when she—'

'I'd like to knock you over with something a lot heavier than a feather,' she muttered.

'Look, you want to hear this or not?'

'Not!' she retorted, then exhaled a sigh weighted with resignation. 'Oh, all right! Go on. I might as well get all the sordid details in one sitting.'

For a moment Jye thought about telling her to blow it out her ear! That if her actions and accusations of the last few minutes were any indication of her opinion of him, then she could go to hell. What changed his mind was the realisation that he didn't want Steff thinking badly of him for even a few minutes.

'Like I said,' he began, 'the last thing I expected was for

Tory to be introduced as Lady Frank Mulligan. Let's face it, Victoria is a fairly common name among the so-called gentry.'

'Whereas *Tory* is just plain common.'

Jye ignored the waspish interjection. 'Anyway, to cut a long, *perfectly innocent* story short, when it became obvious she wasn't about to let something as trivial as her wedding ring stand in the way of a little fling, I decided *I* needed a wife as a deterrent.'

Stephanie produced an ironic laugh. 'You probably think sugar will deter ants too.'

'It was the best idea I could come up with at short notice.'

'Okay. But *why*, when Australia has a population of around nine million women, forty per cent of whom *you* know intimately, did *I* have to get stuck being Mrs Hotstuff Fox?'

'Geez, Steff, give me a break! Who else was I going to get?' he demanded, looking exasperated. 'Apart from the fact I needed someone I could trust and who could think on her feet, if I'd so much as even *thought* the word "marriage", fake or otherwise, in front of most of the women I know, I'd have found myself down the aisle before I could draw another breath!'

'A fate worse than death in your opinion, I know. But couldn't you have told me the whole story before I got dumped in the middle of it.'

'*When?* At the airport? Through the four-way headsets in the helicopter? Be reasonable, Steff. This is the first chance we've had to talk, and as it is I've finished up wearing a drink! How long do you think my credibility would've stood up if you'd started tossing drinks over me in public, huh?'

'Oh, I *see*,' she said with an exaggerated nodding action. '*You're* allowed to be sensitive to humiliation, but I'm not. Talk about double standards!'

'*What is it with all this humiliation stuff?* I haven't done a damn thing to humiliate you! Unless, of course, you mean kissing you at the airport, and if *that* offended you, then you're pretty damned prudish. It sure wouldn't bother the wives of any of my friends.'

'Kiss a lot of your friends' wives breathless, do you?'

'Ha-ha. I meant it wouldn't bother them getting kissed *by their husbands* at an airport. Or anywhere else for that matter.'

'Maybe not, but I bet they'd be *mortified* facing the woman their husband had kissed behind their back. Especially knowing the man-eating witch thought she could do it again!'

'You're upset because *Tory kissed me*?'

'Bingo!'

Expecting to hear a scathing denial, Jye was completely stunned by the admission. 'But *why*? That's stupid. We *aren't* married.'

'I know that! But *Tory* doesn't. And it's obvious she still thinks she has a chance with you. After all, you were once lovers, and as you let her kiss you on the beach it stands to reason she'd assume you still find her attractive.'

'And your point is?'

'Isn't it obvious?'

Jye was honest. 'Not to me.'

Stephanie clearly thought it should have been. With an expression of absolute exasperation on her pretty face, she shook her head, then drew a long, deep breath.

'Look, Jye, pretending to be married and madly in love with my husband is one thing, but pretending to be madly in love with a man who isn't wholly and solely attracted only to me… It's…it's *demeaning*.'

When Jye's only response was to sit mute and stare at her, Stephanie wanted to believe that having been shown the light he was working on an apology. She didn't like fighting with Jye at the best of times, but if they were to successfully thwart Lady Preda-Tory Mulligan he had to understand where she was coming from.

'Well?' she prodded. '*Now* can you understand how embarrassing the whole situation is to me?'

Coal-black eyes merely stared at her for several long, silent seconds before their owner got to his feet, shaking his head and mumbling under his breath.

'Jye... Where are you going?'

'To take a shower and sober up.'

'*Sober up?* You've only had one beer and...' She reached over and shook the can. 'You haven't even finished it.'

'I know. But considering what I've just heard one of us *must* be drunk. Since you found more creative things to do with your gin than drink it...I figure it *has* to be me.'

Stephanie was distracted from the task of putting the finishing touches to her make-up that evening when a man's bathrobe went flying past her to land half-on, half-off the chair by the dressing table. She turned in the direction from which it had travelled to find Jye, leaning negligently in the doorway. He wore an elegant silk shirt and charcoal trousers, but his hair was wet and uncombed and his feet were bare.

'Please don't throw stuff when I'm applying eyeliner; Godfather won't be happy if I make a worker's compensation claim against the company for blinding myself.'

'Sorry.'

He moved to the wardrobe and extracted a pair of shoes. 'Is it going to bother you if I finish getting dressed in here?'

They'd agreed that to avoid the speculation and possible gossip of the resort's housekeepers they'd share the bedroom closet and make it a point to leave bits and pieces of clothing lying around so the room looked as if it was occupied by a happily married couple. However, Stephanie had insisted that Jye would use the bathroom to dress.

'I think my pulse-rate will handle it if you're putting on a pair of shoes and a tie.' She smiled at him via the mirror.

He frowned back. 'This is a holiday resort. You really think I need a tie? I thought I'd get away with just tossing on a sports coat.'

Which of course he would have. In fact, given his in-

credible good looks, athlete-perfect body and an uncon-
scious sense of style even male models would envy,
Stephanie suspected Jye could get away with wearing torn
jeans and a sweatshirt to a Royal wedding. She'd suggested
the tie because she feared the teasing hint of tanned chest
and sinew-delineated neck his shirt currently revealed was
likely to have Tory foaming at the mouth before the entrée
arrived.

'Do you have a shirt with a grandpa-style collar?' she
asked, and received a blank look. '*Oh, you know what I
mean.* One that buttons up to the neck…sort of Nehru-
style.'

Crossing to the wardrobe, he pulled out a roughly woven
linen shirt. 'Like this?'

'Perfect.'

Satisfied she'd now at least get to use her cutlery on the
main course before being required to employ it on Tory in
defence of Jye, she turned back to the mirror and began
applying her mascara. Though the exercise didn't usually
require the same precision as eyeliner, what concentration
it did deserve was shot to hell when the mirror began reflecting the image of a naked male chest. Her hand jerked
as her pulse leapt skyward.

'What are you doing?' she exclaimed, spinning to face
him.

'What you suggested. Switching shirts.'

'But…but…you're supposed to get dressed in the bathroom.'

'For God's sake, Steff, I'm changing my shirt, not my
jocks! It's not like you haven't seen me wearing a lot less
when we've been sailing.'

Knowing he was right had to make her the most *focused*
yachtswoman of all time! *How could she not have noticed
a chest as impressive as the one now on display mere me-
tres from her?* Subtly muscled with a light smattering of
dark hair, it was one of the most touch-tempting things
she'd ever encountered. Oh, boy! She must have been more
upset than she'd realised at the time to have overlooked

such a magnificent sight today, when Jye had been mopping the remnants of her gin and tonic from it. Which, she decided, was a *very good* thing, or she might have succumbed to offering to lick up the spillage! *That* risqué thought had her swallowing hard as she endeavoured to push it aside, yet she couldn't quite bring herself to look away.

'Look, if it bothers you so much, I'll turn around.' Jye matched his words with action. 'Better?'

Stephanie swallowed a groan. To open her mouth was to risk seriously incriminating herself.

'By the way,' he said, slipping on the linen shirt. 'You've got a streak of black stuff down your right cheek.'

'I know that!'

'Hey, don't jump down my throat. I was only trying to be helpful.'

'Sorry.' She pivoted back towards the mirror and reached for the tissues. 'I'm just on edge about tonight, that's all.' It was half the truth.

'Don't be,' he told her. 'You'll do fine. All you've got to do is follow my lead.'

'*Your* lead!' She burst out laughing. 'You've got as much insight into how a married man should behave as you do the lifestyle of a monk!'

She shook her head as she held his gaze via the mirror, 'Oh, no, Jye! You'll take your cues from me, or this charade is going to be blown in two minutes flat.'

He swung his now socked feet onto the waterbed, stretched back. 'Mmm…now this is comfort.' He rocked his body, prompting the mattress into gentle undulation.

'You know, Steff, if you agree to sharing *this*…' he bounced the water-filled mattress again '…with me on a rotation basis, I'll not only agree to take the cues from you, I'll rack them and chalk 'em up for the next game ahead of time.'

Propping himself on one elbow, he gave her a smile that was undoubtedly intended as cajoling but came across as sinfully seductive, causing Stephanie's confused mind to superimpose the image of his bare chest over his now shirt-clad torso and her belly to start mimicking the silken wave motion of the bed. Fortunately it only took a negative shake of her head to correct her vision.

'Forget it, Jye. The bed is mine. And, since you equate acting cues with pool cues, let me put things this way… Marriage is one game where a confirmed bachelor like you is in danger of going in off the black on every shot.'

'Cute. But I should remind you, sunshine, that while you might have aspirations towards matrimony, the reality is you're equally as lacking in hands-on experience as I am.'

'Ah! But unlike you I've studied the subject and have an appreciation of the theories behind it. So it stands to reason that *you* follow my lead. Understand?'

He grinned. 'Would it do me any good if I said no?'

'None at all.'

'In that case I guess you're wearing the pants in this marriage.'

'Precisely. Now, here…' She tossed a comb to him. 'Do your hair.'

'Wonderful,' he grumbled, stretching out his left arm and deftly catching the comb. 'Even in a fake marriage I'm getting nagged at and ordered around.'

'I'm not nagging, I'm being helpful; there's a difference.'

'Right. So tell me, Oh Superior Expert On Marriage, how will *I*, a naive marriage-phobic bachelor, know if I'm making any mistakes tonight?'

'I'll give you a signal. At which point you'll immediately shut up—'

'As any respectable hen-pecked husband would.'

'Then, depending on how badly you blundered, I'll start the appropriate damage control.' She paused and studied the limited pieces of jewellery she'd brought with her.

'I'm not sure what ring I should wear… I've got an emerald one, the pearl one Duncan bought me for my graduation and a sapphire and diamond one I bought myself. Plus three bands that are all etched…'

She turned a questioning frown on him. 'Which one do you think I should wear as a wedding ring?'

'Hell, I don't know! Why ask me?'

'Because then I can at least honestly say *you* picked it out.'

Jye's face creased with amusement. 'You're really getting into this, aren't you?'

Ignoring him, Stephanie picked up a plain, satin finished rose-gold band. 'I've also brought my mother's wedding ring too, but, much as *I* love it, it's too understated to make an impact on Tory.'

'So wear whatever you think *will* make an impact on Tory.'

'Can't, I didn't pack the Hope Diamond this trip.'

Jye stifled a sigh. Sheesh! Steff was acting as if she was *competing* with Tory rather than just trying to keep her at bay and allay any ideas Sir Frank might get that Jye was interested in his wife.

'Steff,' he said wearily, 'is it really going to make a scrap of difference what ring you wear so long as it's on the third finger of your left hand?'

She made a clucking sound with her tongue. '*Yes, Jye it is.* People expect someone as wealthy as you to bestow something dazzling on the woman he loves.'

*But what,* he mused silently, *if the woman in question was someone like Stephanie, who didn't go in for dazzling?*

Irritated at finding himself contemplating something so irrelevant, he attempted to solve what to Steff was apparently a gigantic problem as simply as possible.

'Tell you what,' he said. 'Why not just pick the one *you* like best, and if anyone insinuates I'm tight-fisted, or not suitably devoted to you, I'll simply say you wouldn't settle for anything else, and that when all was said and done I felt it only fitting the choice of ring should be yours, since I was going to make sure you wore it for the rest of your life. Fair enough?'

Stephanie stood statue-still, staring at him with open-mouthed astonishment.

'What?' he said, mentally scrambling to identify where he'd put his foot in it. 'What did I say?'

'Only *the* most romantic thing to ever come out of your mouth, Jye Fox.' She shook her head. 'Who'd have ever thought it...?'

'Hey,' he protested, feeling the need to defend himself against her exaggerated awe. 'I'll have you know I've said plenty of romantic things in my life.'

'I meant while you had clothes on.'

Moments later she stood up, waving her left hand. 'Okay, decision made. Let's go. The sooner this nightmare starts, the sooner it'll be over.'

Jye was pretty sure her jumpsuit was the same one she'd worn to his New Year's Eve party, although when a woman had as many outfits in as many varying shades of yellow as Steff did, it was hard to be absolutely sure. Still, something about the choker neck and the abundance of amber-tinted shoulder it exposed stuck in his mind.

While Stephanie didn't have the lush curves of the women he usually dated, she was perfectly proportioned and carried herself with a poise and grace which turned men's heads without necessarily causing whiplash. He bit back a smile, recalling that the only 'lash' she'd delivered at his party had been to a drunk neighbour who'd been getting overtly friendly with her out on the balcony. Jye had been about to intervene in the situation when Steff, smiling dangerously sweetly, had tugged at the waist of the guy's jeans and deposited the contents of her glass down the front of them.

'I suppose,' he muttered through a grin, 'I should be grateful I only copped the gin and tonic from a distance.'

'What did you say?'

'Huh? Oh, nothing. I was thinking out loud.'

She shot him a highly amused grin. 'Well, it's a start. If we're lucky, and your thinking develops like your reading skills did, one day you'll be able to do it in your head. Then who knows?' she said, looking speculative. 'Maybe one day you'll even feel confident enough not to date women with bust sizes bigger than their IQ and avoid getting caught in farcical situations like this.

'No, don't bother to defend yourself,' she said, when he opened his mouth to do just that. 'I know the speech by heart. *When you're not working you like to keep your commitments to a minimum, your conversations uncomplicated and your companions simple.*'

He grinned unrepentantly. 'Actually, it's the conversation I like simple, not my companions.'

She rolled her eyes. 'If you say so. Now, get off *my* bed and let's go.'

'For someone who's supposedly dreading the evening you're in a damned hurry to leave.' Jye glanced at his watch. 'What's the rush? We aren't due to meet them for another twenty minutes, and it takes less than five to walk to the resort.'

'I know, but if we arrive late it'll look like we got sidetracked in the bedroom.'

'Well, wouldn't that be a *good* thing under the circumstances?' Jye asked, momentarily thrown by her comment and the images that too readily sprang to his mind.

'Uh-uh. Too obvious,' she told him confidently. 'If we'd really been fooling around, we'd try to hide it rather than flaunt it. It'll be better if we're early, so *they* feel obliged to apologise for keeping us waiting. Then we'll dismiss it with something vague but suggestive, like... *"Oh, that's okay. We only got here early because we overslept then rushed like crazy getting ready".*'

Jye sent her an accusing narrow eyed glance. 'You've done this before.'

'Faked being married—never! I just know how a woman like Tory thinks.'

By the time Jye gave up trying to reconcile *that* utterly mind-boggling comment, Stephanie was out of the bedroom and tapping her foot by the front door.

'C'mon, *darling*,' she said, calling him to her with one finger. 'It's important we've had time to settle down in our role before they arrive. We can have a drink at the bar and road-test our routine on the bartender.'

'Sure you don't want us to synchronise our watches?' he

asked drolly. 'Or perhaps we should run through the signals you're going to use so I'll know when I'm saying or doing the wrong thing?' he suggested with pseudo-innocence. 'I mean, given the military-like forward planning you're giving this thing I'd hate to sabotage it by getting *this*...' he stuck his thumbs in his ears and flapped his hands '...confused with *this*...' He crossed his eyes and poked out his tongue.

'Don't worry, Jye,' she told him through a grin. 'I have complete faith in you. Besides, if it looks like you're in danger of accidentally muffing things I'll let you know via a subtle kick in the shins or a nudge in the ribs.'

'Well, I suppose a *subtle* kick to the shins beats having an ice bucket tipped over my head,' he muttered.

'I swear I won't resort to the ice bucket unless it's *absolutely* necessary.'

She'd been chuckling as he guided her out of the door and turned to lock it, so her suddenly gasped four-letter word caught him off guard. But before he could do more than half turn to see what was wrong she was using her body to pin him against the door.

'*Man-eater at two o'clock,*' she whispered urgently. '*Stay cool!*'

The next thing Jye knew, he was being thoroughly kissed!

## CHAPTER FIVE

BE COOL! She had to be kidding! Jye felt as if he was a heartbeat away from total meltdown. What the hell had happened to the closed-mouthed, rigid, unresponsive woman he'd kissed at the airport?

'Gosh, I hope I'm not interrupting anything.'

Jye doubted the sound of Tory's voice would have registered with him had it not been for the fact it triggered the withdrawal of the ardent mouth and warm body pressing against his own. But, even as his shellshocked system struggled to regain its equilibrium, the woman responsible for his emotional drunkenness seemed remarkably unaffected.

'Not at all, Lady Mulligan,' Stephanie said, adding in a loud stage whisper to Jye. '*See*, I told you we only had time for a quickie.'

He supposed, given the distance separating them, Tory might have interpreted the strangled sound he made at that remark as a muttered endearment to his 'wife', but the look on Steff's face, and the way she seized his hand and dragged him down the path to where Tory stood beside a golf buggy, was clearly a message to *get with the programme*!

'I'm sorry, Tory,' he said, rallying. 'Did we get the arrangements wrong? I was sure Sir Frank said we'd meet in the bar at seven-thirty.'

Tory's hand fluttered to rest reassuringly on Jye's arm. 'Oh, no, Jye! You're absolutely right! I just thought I'd pick you up in a buggy, in case you had trouble locating the resort.'

'Oh, you take those little signposts we passed on the way here down at night, do you?' Stephanie thought she'd phrased the question with superb innocence, but when her elbow was squeezed by a male hand she smiled again, gave

58

a vapid laugh and dutifully said, 'No, really, Lady Victoria, it was very thoughtful of you to volunteer to *chauffeur* us.'

This earned her another disapproving squeeze from Jye; there was just no pleasing some people.

'Yes, it was,' Tory agreed, smirking. 'But unfortunately, Stephanie, you'll have to sit in the back. Jye would be far too cramped in such a confined space…he's got such *long* legs. Honestly, being tall can be such a curse at times. You've no idea how fortunate you are to be so short.'

Even without the three-inch heels she was wearing Stephanie's five-four didn't exactly qualify her as a pygmy, and she barely restrained herself from pointing out that Tory was equally *fortunate* in that being almost six foot allowed *her* the luxury of getting away with too many extra pounds and a surplus of silicone! However, the desire not to lower herself to Tory's bitchy level had her pasting an unconcerned smile on her face and dutifully hopping into the back of the buggy. Tory waited until Jye had taken his place in the front seat before *slithering* in beside him, making the most of the hem-to-armpit split in her dress. Stephanie wasn't sure if she was more nauseated or amused by the woman's blatant exhibitionism.

*And Jye had actually had an affair with this woman?*

Sheesh! He'd dated his share of hard-nosed bitches and intellectual tragedies in his time, but if Tory Mulligan wasn't the worst… Well, it was a good thing Jye was anti-marriage, because the idea of him producing offspring with any of his romantic liaisons would be the best argument for zero population growth ever.

*This*, Stephanie decided later, was proving to be the longest night of her life and the sad thing was they hadn't even started the main course yet!

It didn't take a genius to recognise that Sir Frank was so stupidly besotted with his third wife, or at least her physical attributes, that he was oblivious to the fact *her* sights were well and truly fixed on Jye. Whenever Sir Frank's gaze strayed to his wife's overexposed breasts, which were constantly heaving, presumably with the strain of breathing in her tight dress, Preda-Tory was sending sultry looks across the table to Jye.

'Jye tells me you've been married for six months,' Sir Frank said, as he topped up her champagne glass, then completely refilled his own. How do *you* cope being married to a man as busy as Jye? I know Victoria always says she has a hell of a time when I'm away on business, and finds it terribly hard to amuse herself.'

*Wanna bet?* Stephanie retorted silently.

'Well, as you know, Sir Frank, I work for Porter's too, so I'm usually kept pretty busy myself,' she said.

'Truth be known,' Jye put in, 'Steff works way too hard. I was the lonely one when she was in Western Australia. Which,' he added, bestowing a wide smile in her direction, 'is why I was so delighted when she agreed to join me here.'

'Naturally, you being Duncan Porter's goddaughter…'

The moment the words were out of Tory's mouth Stephanie began preparing to defend herself from a nepotism jibe, but the sly brunette threw one in from left field.

'…I imagine you must've had a big wedding.'

Caught off guard, Stephanie was a trifle slow saying, 'No, it was a small, quiet affair.'

Which unfortunately had her answer clashing with Jye's, 'Yes, we were married in St Mary's Cathedral.'

The conflicting responses predictably had Tory smirking like a Cheshire cat. 'Really?' she said, with a sceptically arched eyebrow. 'At the cathedral?'

'Eh, yes. Steff's Catholic,' Jye put in quickly. 'And she'd *always said* she wanted to be married with a nuptial mass. Naturally, not being not overly religious myself, I was happy to go along with something Stephanie's *always* felt so strongly about.'

Fortunately neither Mulligan seemed to pick up on the subtle nuance in Jye's tone which promised she was going to pay for not sticking with her often-voiced plans for her *oh, so perfect* wedding on this occasion.

Sir Frank broke into hearty laughter. 'Well, son, with the experience of three marriages behind me, I say you made the right choice, Jye.' He sent a *'just between us men'* wink to the younger man. 'Give in on the things that don't matter to you and stick to your guns and choose your *gifts* wisely when it comes to getting the upper hand on the things that do.'

Apparently unperturbed by her husband's tactless reference to her predecessors, and the implication his wife's co-operation could be bought, Tory produced a too knowing smile and turned it full force onto Stephanie. *Again.*

'While I can *appreciate* Jyc's...er, *thoughtfulness and sensitivity*, I'm still a little confused...'

Wishing she could replace the confusion with concussion, Stephanie waited for the knock-out punch.

'I know St Mary's Cathedral is considered *the* place for a lot of high society Roman Catholic weddings, but it's the *largest* church in Sydney. Hardly what *I* would've chosen for... How did you describe it, Stephanie? "A small, quiet affair"?'

'You're quite right, Lady Mulligan. St Mary's is more famous for large society weddings,' Stephanie agreed, unblinkingly meeting the other woman's gaze. 'Which is why my parents chose to be married there. However, despite the size and grandeur of the cathedral, Jye and I invited only our very closest friends. For us, everything about our wedding was a sentimental decision rather than a social or practical one.'

The smoothly delivered lie won her a congratulatory pat on the knee from Jye, under the cover of their small circular table.

'A touching gesture,' Sir Frank observed in a quiet voice. 'You're probably unaware of this, Victoria,' he continued, 'but both Jye's and Stephanie's parents died in the same tragic accident. It shocked all of us in the resort industry at the time.'

'You knew my father, Sir Frank?'

'Oh, not personally, my dear. But within the industry he

was widely regarded as a young man going places. As, of course, was yours, Jye,' he added quickly. 'The rivalry between two of Duncan Porter's brightest and most ambitious young executives was watched widely by head-hunters within our ranks looking to strengthen their own organisations.' He smiled. 'But, to the disappointment of everyone, the two of them were exclusively loyal to Duncan.' He shook his head. 'It's a tragedy they both died so young. And at the same time... Tsk, tsk.'

Jye mentally willed Stephanie to lift her downcast lashes, so he could get some idea of what she was feeling. There'd been no missing the eagerness in her voice when Sir Frank had mentioned her father and while he had no illusions as to exactly how ruthlessly ambitious *his* parents had been, he had no idea how Steff remembered hers. Four years younger than him, she had been only six when the motor cruiser on which the four of them had been entertaining foreign hoteliers had exploded. With the exception of Stephanie's mother, all on board had been killed instantly; Felicia Worthington had died in hospital two days later.

Only now did it occur to Jye that Steff and he had never discussed their parents in all the years they'd spent growing up together in Duncan's care. While he had no doubts Duncan loved them both dearly, the crusty old bachelor had never been one to encourage displays of emotion or sentiment. He wondered now if that had been a good or bad thing for someone with the naturally emotive personality of Steff, who as a six-year-old girl had flatly refused to leave the bedside of her dying mother until she'd taken her last breath.

Glancing at the simple rose-gold ring adorning Steff's left hand, he realised there was a lot he didn't know about this woman, and suddenly he wanted to...very much.

The main course came and went in an atmosphere rife with lies, innuendos, suspicion, unconcealed lust and the seemingly non-stop popping of champagne corks. Stephanie felt as if she was in a scene from a poorly scripted but lavishly produced soap opera, and that she was the only one emerging with any acting credibility.

As the copious quantities of French champagne Sir Frank single-handedly disposed of took an ever stronger grip on him, the less inclined he was to elevate his eyes above the level of his wife's cleavage; or notice she was gradually edging her chair nearer to Jye's. Any attempt to refocus the man's mind on business was dismissed with remarks such as, 'Let's save that for the office.' Or, 'My Victoria gets distressed when I put business ahead of her.'

Frankly, Stephanie was all for *anything* that would distress 'his Victoria', who'd manoeuvred her chair to a point where she was close enough to play footsies with Jye. She *knew* this because, only moments ago, she'd had the startling but eminently gratifying experience of intercepting a wayward *bare* female foot with the heel of her shoe! Naturally, in a truly inspired piece of acting, she'd drowned out Tory's yelp of pain in a flurry of profuse apologies and the excuse that she'd kicked out to try and rid herself of a cramp.

'Obviously you have poor circulation,' Tory had replied with narrow-eyed hatred. 'You should eat more salt.' A malicious smile emerged on her face. 'Although at your age it could be the sign of something more insidious.'

'Oh? I always thought salt was bad for you. Not that I'm questioning you, Lady Mulligan,' she'd added, with respectful earnestness. 'I know that with your *superior age and experience* you're far more of an expert on the subject of *circulation* than I am.'

Of course for *that* mild little retort she'd had Jye scowling at her as well. Talk about a lack of gratitude! Just because he wanted Porter's to win this deal, it didn't mean he should expect her to let herself be annihilated by the original she-devil without a modicum of resistance! *He* might be naive enough to believe that merely producing a wife would protect him from Preda-Tory, but she wasn't! Why, even now he was letting the woman draw him into a conversation about boats, as if he believed the innocuous content of the conversation meant she'd given up the idea of pursuing him.

'You know, Frank…' Tory said, refilling her husband's champagne glass, although it was half empty again before the bottle was back in the ice bucket. 'We really must organise ourselves to get out on the water with Jye while he's here. It's obvious he loves sailing, and we don't use the cruiser nearly enough.'

Sir Frank's slurred response didn't allow Stephanie to point out the difference between a yacht and a motor cruiser.

'S'at's 'cause I'm too busy in th'office, Pea…shez. ''N when I'm not…' He jiggled his eyebrows. 'We're bofth too busy, eh?'

Stephanie couldn't even raise a dutiful smile when the old man nudged her in the ribs, trying unsuccessfully to wink. She wasn't prudish by a long chalk, but any opportunity to discuss business had deteriorated in direct proportion to Sir Frank's ability to control either his drinking or his flirtatious wife. She'd kept hoping Jye would call an end to the night, but as best she could tell he didn't appear perturbed by the futility of the past few hours; although he had sent her a few *'help me out, here'* looks during the last twenty minutes.

Of course it would have helped if she'd had some idea of exactly *how* he wanted her to do that. Since Tory hadn't yet reached the stage of climbing into his lap and ripping his clothes off, at this point, as appealing as the notion was, tipping the ice bucket on the other woman's head might be viewed as an act of aggression. Unless…

Jye almost bit off his tongue from the surprise and impact of Steff's shoe connecting with his shin! It took a mammoth effort to hold back a blistering expletive and turn his grimace of pain into what at best came out as a mangled smile. His eyes were watering as he met her innocent-looking ones.

'Jye, honey…I'd really *love* to dance.'

Sorely tempted, *particularly in the region of his left calf,* to tell her she should've thought of that *before* she crippled him, Jye hesitated for split second, trying to gauge if he could even walk without hobbling.

'Oh, *please, darling...*' She practically purred the endearment as she walked her fingernails across the back of his hand with a seductive effectiveness that overpowered the painful throb of his left leg and sensitised higher placed sections of his anatomy.

Her smile was pure temptress. 'After all this is *our song.*'

'Our song', he realised, was Dr Hook's very suggestive 'I'm Gonna Love You A Little Bit More'. Hoping he was doing a better job of hiding his amusement than Tory was her irritation at his sluggish pick-up of Steff's obvious escape ploy, Jye got to his feet.

'Of course, sweetheart. I just realised that myself.' Taking Steff's hand, he smiled at their dinner companions. 'If you'll excuse—?'

'Shertainly, shertainly!' Sir Frank encouraged. 'I'm a bith pash dancing myself, but I can still appreciate the 'traction of a booful woman in my arms.'

'More like the old sleaze appreciates having a woman flat on her back,' Steff muttered as they stepped onto the dimly lit dance floor.

'Or perhaps...' he grinned '...flat out on the floor.'

'Oh, knock it off! If I didn't get away from the pair of them I was going to throw up! My God, he's ogling her like a horny sixteen-year-old. *Not that she's any better!*' she told him hotly. 'She's thrusting her boobs in his face at the same time she's coming on to you! And you're encouraging her, damn it!'

'I'm doing no such thing! The most I've done is talk to her.'

'*Exactly!*'

'Be reasonable, Steff, I can't very well ignore her. Besides, flirting is only a game to Tory. Sure, she might like to win, but the most important thing is the chase.'

'Really?' she said with a sardonic stare. 'Well, in case

you haven't noticed her *baying*, she's currently hunting Fox!'

Jye was genuinely amused, but, while he'd always appreciated Steff's wit, he was only now becoming aware that he'd been short-sighted when it came to other things about her. For starters, how seductively her body surrendered to the rhythm of the music.

Because she was disposed to letting her emotions rule her head, Jye knew that in times of stress working to a predetermined plan never came easily to Stephanie. The wider implication of that being that, given her annoyance and preoccupation with the Mulligans, it was unlikely she was currently giving any conscious thought to her pseudo-role of happily married woman, and therefore the fluidity and ease with which she was moving with him around the dance floor had to be instinctive. It was a concept more arousing than interesting, since her slight but tantalising curves were melded against him in a way that fired his baser instincts.

'*Jye*…are you paying attention to me?'

'More than ever.'

'Good. Then *don't* let your guard down with Tory.'

She sighed, and the rise of her breasts against him kicked his pulse-rate up another notch. 'For some reason men have a habit of underestimating what a woman's capable of.'

*Tell me about it,* he thought, his fingers itching to discover if the skin of her throat felt as smooth as her bare shoulders.

'Stop worrying, Steff. I'll be able to stay ahead of Tory. Although, for the record, she's the type who if she gets ticked off could turn around and say something to Sir Frank and deliberately screw the deal as a way of getting even.'

'I should be *surprised*?'

'All I'm saying is it'd be wiser if you stopped provoking her every time you opened your cute little mouth.'

Her eyes widened. '*Me?* Provoking *her*! Jye Fox, have you been wearing earplugs all night, or what? *She* hasn't let up taking potshots at me since she picked us up. *I* haven't done one thing to deliberately stir *her* up,' she avowed righteously.

'Really? Then if that unnecessary kiss outside the cabin wasn't designed to provoke *her*, I guess it was meant to get me stirred up?'

'Did it—? I mean, don't be ridiculous! For heaven's sake, that kiss was every bit as necessary and no worse than the one you gave me at the airport!'

'I'll agree with you on one point,' he said, intrigued by the sudden flush to her cheeks and the over-zealous denial. 'It definitely wasn't *worse* than the airport clinch. In fact, I'd have to say your technique improved in leaps and bounds in just a few hours.'

'*Excuse me?*'

'Well, there was a wealth of difference between the closed-mouthed unresponsive statue I kissed at the airport and the woman who flattened me against the door of the cabin.'

'Well…eh, that's because I wasn't *catatonic with shock* at the cabin. By *then* I knew what was going on.'

*Well, at least that makes one of us,* Jye thought, because *he* sure as hell hadn't known what had hit him! From the instant her mouth had touched his, he'd felt as if he'd been electrocuted. Perhaps that was only the result of being caught off guard by Stephanie's actions, and not having a chance to take control of the situation before she'd drawn away, but it irked him that she'd blind-sided him like that. Gazing down at her slightly parted lips, he wondered if repeating the exercise would prove conclusively whether it had been the woman or the circumstances which were responsible for the sending of his pulse into orbit.

When his thumb, of its own volition, grazed her lower lip just as she nervously moistened it with her tongue, Jye knew he had to find out. But this time he didn't want either one of them to have the excuse of being caught unawares.

Stephanie couldn't contain her tiny gasp of amazement as Jye lowered his head and began nuzzling the pulse beneath her ear, and, had the arm encircling her waist not tightened at that precise instant, she'd have doubtless sunk to the floor. Struggling to rise above her body's chaotic response to his too convincing performance of a loving husband, she tried unsuccessfully to ease back a little.

'Eh... Jye... Um...aren't you overdoing...it a tad?' she managed to croak.

'Shh,' he whispered, then, recalling her earlier words added, *'Be cool.'*

*Be cool!* she thought frantically. He had to be kidding! Didn't he have *any* idea of the effect he was having on her? Hell, from the moment he'd taken her into his arms she'd barely been able to breathe, and now... Sheesh! Her heart was pounding as if it was going to burst through her chest, and she was heating up so fast she was beginning to sweat in places that weren't affected by room temperature. The scent of his aftershave was as evocative and sensually stirring as incense merging with steam, and just rolling her tongue around her mouth conjured up the taste of the earlier kiss.

*No, Stephanie!* her brain screamed. *Stop rolling your tongue, right this minute!*

Hell! What was happening here? Well, okay...so she wasn't so innocent as to not recognise her hormones were giving her a wake up call, but for heaven's sake this was *Jye!* She'd danced with him hundreds of times and not been turned on by him! Albeit he'd never actually nibbled on her ear or moved his hand over her butt in the sexy, stimulating way he was doing now. Mentally she fought to hang onto the fact that what he was doing was purely a show for the Mulligans' benefit. It wasn't easy.

*Whoa!* The things he was making her feel!

She supposed she must have been this aroused before...maybe. But *not* fully clothed, vertical and in public! And he hadn't even *kissed* her yet. Lord, if he did that— *and she wished to hell he'd quit dilly-dallying with her neck and get to it!*—boy, they'd have to start hosing her down and—

'Steff...' Though his moist lips barely skimmed her skin,

his breath nevertheless sent a shower of goosebumps along her spine, making her shiver with delight. He continued to nibble and talk. 'You...mmm...haven't answered my... question yet.'

*He'd asked her a question?* When? More importantly, *what?* Was it *the* question, or just something mundane like, Who do you think is going to win the NBL title this year?

She supposed she could always answer, *I'm not sure.* Then, depending on whether he started promising to *be gentle* with her or quoting rebound and shooting statistics, she could pick it up from there.

'Steff?'

'Um, eh...I'm not sure,' she said huskily, and felt him chuckle against her.

'It wasn't that hard a question.'

'It wasn't? Oh. Well, actually I— *Oh, my God!*'

In unison with Steff's horrified gasp, all colour drained from her face, and as she slumped against Jye as if her legs had given way he knew real panic for the first time in his life.

*'Steff, what's wrong?'* There was no verbal response as she burrowed against him, pressing her face into his chest. 'Stephanie? Honey, what is it? Are you sick? Do you—?'

Her head shook furiously against him, before angling to furtively glance over his shoulder. Jerking back, she mumbled something incomprehensible, then repeated her action, shoving him slightly to the left, as if using him as a shield. She was rigid with tension.

'For God's sake, Steff,' he hissed, grasping her shoulders. *'What's wrong?'*

'I hate to tell you this, Jye, but our marriage is over.' Wide grey eyes stared into his. 'Brad Carey just stepped into the elevator...'

The words hit Jye like a kick to the guts.

## CHAPTER SIX

'YOU are not ending this marriage, Stephanie, and that's final!'

Tossing the cabin key on the table with a force that caused it to slide across the pine surface and bounce at her feet, Jye stalked to the bar. Grateful for anything that provided her with a few extra seconds to gather her wits in the face of Jye's unexpected fury, she stooped down and picked up the key.

Self-control, Duncan had always told them, was the most crucial element in retaining the upper hand in all situations. Living up to that motto had never been easy for her, despite the ease with which Jye and her godfather had adhered to it. Or at least Jye had until now. She couldn't recall ever seeing him so ticked off. Usually she was the one flying off the handle while he remained stoically calm to the point of indifference.

Admittedly he'd initially taken the news in his normal unflappable stride, explaining to the seriously plastered Sir Frank and his suspicious wife that Stephanie was unwell and he was anxious to get her home. All *her* role had required of her at that time was to remain silent, wan-looking, and allow Jye to support her limp body. Had any Hollywood talent scouts been present they'd have signed her on the spot. The only thing was, she hadn't been acting—more like paralysed with shock by Brad's unexpected appearance. The trek from the resort back to the cabin had been little more than a blur of tropical vegetation to her, but then again at the speed Jye had dragged her along the narrow path, muttering under his breath, she figured they had pole position all sewn up for the next Grand Prix.

'I mean it, Stephanie! We're staying married. *End of story!*'

'Jye, you know Brad being here changes everything.' She ignored the murderous look in his dark eyes as he viciously twisted the cap off a long-necked bottle of beer. 'We have to discuss this rationally. All three of us.'

His hand faltered, halting the beer bottle mid-way to his mouth. '*Three* of us? Aren't you forgetting someone?'

She frowned. 'Who?'

'The name *Karrie Dent* ring any...*wedding bells*, with you, Steff?'

'Karrie's not here.'

A cruel, ironic laugh escaped him before he took a long swig and lowered the bottle to the bar-top. 'Sure of that, are you?'

'Yes. Brad was by himself.'

'Oh, wake up to yourself! That doesn't mean his *wife* wasn't stripped and between the sheets waiting for him upstairs.' He smirked. 'Does it?'

'Jye—'

'*Does it, Steff?*' he repeated. 'You might want to believe Carey's marriage isn't a...' he used his hands as inverted commas '""...real marriage"', but you can't *know* that for sure. Can you? *Can you*, Steff?'

'All right! If it makes you happy, Jye, then, *yes*! I suppose it is possible that Karrie was upstairs!'

He lifted the bottle to her in a mock toast. 'More than possible, if I know Carey.'

'That's just it, Jye! *You* don't know him.'

Drawing a steadying breath, she reminded herself it was only natural Jye would be upset over the inevitable loss of the Illusion deal. It wasn't going to do any good for them both to start ranting and raving; she had to be the rational one. Although that was easier said than done, since she wasn't a saint and the urge to shove a beer bottle down someone's throat *horizontally* was getting stronger by the minute.

'Look, Jye,' she said, amazed she could sound so calm. 'Even if Karrie was upstairs...it doesn't change anything.'

'Doesn't change anything! Why, you damned hypocrite!'

Shock and outrage had her fumbling for words. 'I…I… I'm no such thing! How dare—'

'Well, what do *you* call a person who lampoons someone for something then turns around and announces she's going to do the same thing herself?' he challenged.

'Who did I lampoon?'

'Tory! But never mind that…' The bottle was waved airily. 'Let's try this one… *What do you call someone who promises to do something for someone then backs out when they find something they'd like to be doing better?* Huh?' he demanded. 'Or someone who turns her back on the man who raised her the one and only time he's really counting on *her*? What, Steff?'

'You're not being fair! I'm not to blame because this'll cost Duncan the deal! *You're* the one who wanted us to pretend to be married!'

'Yeah, but I'm *not* the one ending things because I'm hot for a married man!'

The viciously flung accusation seemed to reverberate through the room, and Jye knew he'd said too much when Steff didn't instantly hit back with some sarcastic remark. Damn! What was wrong with him? He was making an absolute hash of this. The situation called for logical regrouping, but, instead of wading in the shallow end of the problem, he'd allowed his temper to plunge them in the deep end. What disturbed him even more was that in the absence of a denial, Steff was mutely letting them sink.

She stood staring at him with eyes that were shadowed by hurt. It was obvious she really cared for Carey. But, hell, couldn't she just lie for the sake of argument? Steff never backed down from a good argument with him.

Of course she never lied to him either. Not about the things that mattered, and the insane proposal she'd put to him the other day was proof Carey mattered. The realisation brought a surge of conflicting emotions Jye didn't entirely understand, but he understood guilt. And right now it was tearing at his guts for hurting Stephanie.

'I'm sorry, Steff. That was a low blow.'

The reality was he was sorry for a whole lot more than that, yet to admit any of the things going round in his head right at this minute wouldn't help the situation. Tonight had been a shock to his system even before Brad bloody Carey had been chucked into the equation. That his only thought out on that dance floor had been whether or not Stephanie had ever fantasised about making love to him the way he'd suddenly found himself imagining doing it to her had him more strung out than he'd ever felt. So strung out, in fact, that when he was in desperate need of a drink here he was sucking on an imported beer he hated because, *damn it all to hell*, his taste buds were stalled in flashback mode and tasting Steff's kiss!

He dumped the foreign beer down the sink and bent to the mini-fridge to retrieve a preferred brand. It was at times like these he wished he drank Scotch! He felt wired and edgy, and was practically choking on frustration that wasn't entirely sexual; although taking a particularly irritating platinum blonde to bed would go close to alleviating about ninety per cent of it! On that worrying thought, he reached into the fridge and snagged a beer.

The loud, unexpected peal of female of laughter had him jerking his head up with no thought for the bar's overhang. 'Owww!'

'Good!' came a callous cheer. 'Serves you right!'

Stephanie's face wore a smirk of malicious satisfaction, which caused him to think she'd been reading his mind a few seconds ago. *Oh, great,* he thought, clamping his hand to the throbbing spot above his right ear.

'Bleeding?' she asked as he lowered his hand and inspected it.

'Sorry to disappoint you. A headache's probably the best you can hope for.'

'Maybe a headache will dull that over-active libido of yours that puts a sexual slant on *everything*,' she muttered.

*Cripes!* She *had* read his mind!

'Put the bottle on it.'

He blinked. 'Huh?'

'The coldness will stop it swelling.'

'*My libido?*'

She sniggered. 'Yeah, right! Antarctica couldn't manage *that*. I meant *your head*.'

'Oh, right,' he said, taking her advice and wincing at the contact. 'Explain.'

'The cold will stop—'

'*Not that.* Explain what the hell you found so funny a moment ago.'

'Oh…just your assumption that I was backing out of our "marriage" because I'm hot for Brad.' Her eyes fixed on him like lasers. 'I never said that.'

'You said—'

'I know *exactly* what I said,' she told him haughtily. 'And it wasn't *that*. You misunderstood.'

'I misunderstood, "*I hate to tell you this, Jye, but our marriage is over. Brad Carey just stepped into the elevator*"?'

'Yes!' she snapped. 'You did!'

She crossed the floor, scowling. 'Let me see your head.'

There was no evident sympathy in her voice, but her eyes were definitely softer. Removing the bottle, he bent his head forward, and a second later her fingers moved tentatively though his hair to glide over the small bump. The tingling sensation shooting down his spine might have been caused by the knock, but if so his hormones must have been concussed too, because they were definitely in Disneyland!

Grey-blue eyes looked deeply into his as she continued to caress his skull. Lord, with a touch like hers she could probably perform open-heart surgery without anaesthetic. 'Is it very sore?' she asked, concern softening her voice as her fingertips gently probed his skull. 'It doesn't feel very swollen.'

*Keep that up and it soon will be!* 'No?' he responded dully, then cleared his throat. 'It feels like hell.' Actually, heaven was a better comparison, but Jye hadn't been knocked entirely stupid.

Frowning, she removed the cold bottle from his hand and

gently held it against his injury. The action brought her closer, and being sandwiched between her soft curves and the bar reactivated the memory of how she'd felt moulded against him on the dance floor.

'The point is, Jye,' she said, obviously having no idea of the effect she was having on him, 'Brad Carey *knows* I'm not married to you or anyone else.'

'Mmm.' He breathed deeply again, trying to identify her perfume, which was evocatively wrapping itself around his senses. 'So?'

Her focus shifted from his head to his face, her impatience evident not just in the noisy way she banged the bottle to the bar, but in her expression as she brought her face to within a few inches of his.

'*So,*' she said. 'We might be able to con Sir Lush and Lady Lust, but *not* Brad. Are you beginning to grasp anything of what I'm saying here?'

The only thing Jye wanted to grasp at that moment was her! Put his hands on her hips, haul her against him and lave those tightly pursed lips with his tongue until they parted for him. Unfortunately he spent too long dwelling on the subsequent delights of such an action instead of executing it, and suddenly she was halfway across the room again, raking her hair with agitation and looking about as physically aware of Jye as she was the floor rug she was pacing so precisely.

'I can't believe Brad picked *this* resort to come to,' she muttered. 'Hell, I can't believe we thought we could get away with it even if he hadn't!'

'Steff... Look, this can still work.'

'Give it up, Jye. We've been caught in our own devious web and—'

'Not yet, we haven't been.'

Stephanie sighed. When it came to business, with the exception of Duncan, Jye was the most single-minded person she knew. Which was probably a good thing, considering how unbusinesslike *she'd* been feeling around him this evening. In the past she'd accepted his good looks as easily as she accepted night followed day, but in less than twenty-four hours Jye's sex appeal suddenly seemed hotter and more blinding than the sun. God forgive her for being so traitorous to Duncan and the Porter Corporation, but to her personally Brad's arrival was like having a pair of sunglasses and a bottle of SPF 30 dropped in her lap.

'Steff, listen… I'm sure we can work out a way if we just put our heads together.'

His clichéd phrase threw up an image that had nothing to do with intellectual collaboration and skated way too close to copulation for her to do anything else but shake her head vigorously.

In less time than it took for one of her erratic heartbeats to stop and another to start, he'd closed the space between them and was holding her shoulders.

'C'mon, Steff, you know how important this is to Duncan,' he cajoled. 'All his life he's had his heart set on getting hold of an island. It'll kill him if he misses this opportunity.'

'That…that's emotional blackmail,' she stammered, as his hands moved to her neck, angling her head to look up at him. She'd felt much safer staring at the second button of his shirt rather than into the liquid depths of his intense black eyes. 'Um…he'll be disappointed, I admit, but we can't help that.'

'Yes, we can,' he insisted, his proximity and touch causing her hormones to suggest moves that would have made Tory look shy around men.

'You're surrendering too easily, Steff.'

*Which showed what he knew!* Right now she was fighting the battle of her life against temptations she'd never expected to feel around Jye. He was practically family; there was no precedence for the way the heat of his hands on her bare flesh was beginning to melt her from the inside.

*'I'm being sensible.'* Had truer words ever been spoken? she wondered, as she pulled away from him. 'There's no way we can pull this off now. It was a crazy idea to begin with, but now it's impossible.'

'Steff, *please*? Hear me out. We just need to think about this calmly.'

*Easy for him to talk about being calm! He wasn't two heartbeats from stripping off his clothes and throwing himself at her!* Maybe she was drunk? It didn't seem likely, on the few glasses of champagne she'd had, but as a way of explaining what she was feeling it would make a great lifeline.

'Why don't I fix us a drink and we can sit down and consider our options?'

If she'd thought she was vulnerable to him on the dance floor, it was nothing compared to how she felt now. So remaining in his proximity and putting more alcohol into a body already intoxicated on his sheer masculinity was lunacy. She needed space and she needed it *now*.

'I don't want a drink. And I don't think you're supposed to drink after a head injury.'

'Well…okay, then. How about I make us some coffee and—'

'*No, Jye! I don't want anything!*' Feeling a fool for the edge of hysteria in her reply, she paused and sucked in a deep breath before adopting a more rational and composed tone. 'Look, I agree that for Duncan's sake at least we should talk this through—'

'Good. Then—'

'Not tonight, Jye. It's late and I'm too tired to think right now. Okay?'

Jye felt anything *but* tired. And to be perfectly honest *thinking* was the last thing he wanted her to start doing! He was damn certain she hadn't been thinking on the dance floor, at least not until that jerk Carey had shown up. A fresh wave of fury hit him. What the hell did she see in the cretin anyway?

At the sound of her heavy sigh he mentally regrouped and looked up to find her standing in the doorway of the bedroom. 'Sorry, what did you say?'

'I said, we'll talk in the morning. Goodnight, Jye.'

She closed the door before he had a chance to respond,

but a few minutes later, as he stood staring balefully at the sofa he'd finally managed to open out, she re-emerged hugging a pillow to her.

'Don't look so glum,' she told him, a wry smile on her now make-up-free face. 'Who knows? Maybe after a good night's sleep we *will* be able to figure out a way to keep us in the bidding for the resort.'

'Easy for you to say,' he muttered. 'You aren't the one who has to sleep on this mattress of misery.'

'You're right. And, since this whole marriage thing was *your* idea, I could be *really* mean and say that you made your bed and you shouldn't complain about lying in it. However, I won't...' Rank mischief shone in her eyes a fraction before her whole face lit up with a grin. *''Cause there are no spare sheets!'*

Jye swore. 'You're kidding, right?'

'Nope. But the good news is, you do get a pillow. Here, catch!'

The pillow hit him in the face at the same instant the bedroom door banged shut.

Stephanie squinted at the bedside clock, then rolled over, refusing to acknowledge the banging on the bedroom door. Thoughts of Jye had kept her awake half the night as it was, and she'd be damned if she was going to let him drag her out of bed at this ungodly hour. Although the tidal wave which suddenly hit the mattress beneath her went close to pitching her over the side.

'What the—?' A hand was clamped over her mouth.

'*Shh!*' Jye's whisper was urgent. His unshaven face alarmed. *And his magnificent body bare!* Well, from the waist up at any rate; Stephanie didn't dare look lower.

'Keep your voice down,' he warned her.

Grabbing his wrist, she pulled his hand down. 'How did you get in here? I locked the door.'

'I know. I had to come through the bathroom. 'He frowned. 'Why'd you lock—? No, never mind that; there's someone at the door.'

'So...*answer*...it.'

He gave her a *'don't start'* look, then swore as the banging started up again. Much louder.

'Listen, Steff, did Carey see you last night?'

She shook her head, more to clear it than anything else, but Jye chose to take it as a negative response.

'Okay, then our charade hasn't been blown yet, so let's assume that's Tory at the front door—'

'Couldn't we start the day on a bright note and assume it's the Grim Reaper?'

Jye rolled off the bed, *mercifully wearing a pair of boxers.* 'I've already thrown the sofa back together, but it'll be better if you answer the door and see what she wants.'

'You mean you haven't worked that out *yet*? Boy, are you slow on the uptake.'

Ignoring her sarcasm, he tossed her the shirt he'd worn the night before. 'Put this on,' he said, his eyes flicking over her with disapproval. 'A Sydney Swans' football jersey isn't exactly suggestive of a night of passion.'

'Funny,' she said, snatching the shirt from him. 'That's not what the original owner said when he gave it to me.' Well satisfied with the scowl that remark brought to his handsome face, Stephanie darted into the bathroom and hastily swapped the jersey for the shirt, determined to ignore the hint of Jye's cologne it carried.

The shirt's hem hit her about mid-thigh and actually covered more of her than what she'd just shed. The banging re-started, but this time it also came from the door leading to her bedroom.

'Hurry it up, Steff!'

'I'm trying to, damn it!' she retorted, fiddling with the shirt's buttons and artfully arranging the neck in the hope of appearing sexy. Unfortunately she hadn't developed a cleavage overnight.

*'Coming!'* she called, exiting the bathroom and deciding that if Jye wanted to go down fighting, she'd play along. But sooner or later Brad's presence was going to cause his plan to unravel at a light speed.

As she reached the front door she forced a sing-song cheerfulness into her voice. *'Whoooo is it?'*

'Lady Mulligan,' came the curt reply.

*Surprise, surprise!* she thought, pulling both the door and her false smile wider. 'Well, good morning, Lady Mulligan! How are you? Gosh, isn't it just a *gorgeous* day?'

As the woman's eyes rudely surveyed her from head to foot Stephanie returned the insult and decided it was probably one of the rare occasions that Tory had been in the position of being over-dressed. While the brunette's knit top and painted on shorts didn't leave much to the imagination, they weren't quite so suggestive as a man's shirt with nothing underneath it. Not that the shirt was transparent, but with Tory's mind it didn't need to be.

'Is Jye here? I need to speak with him.'

'Well, *yes*, he's here…but, eh, he's not exactly dressed for company…*if* you know what I mean.'

'Then I'll wait…' Magnificent white teeth were bared in a snarl. *'If* you don't mind?'

Stephanie *did* mind. And she was very tempted to—

'Who is it, babe?'

Pivoting at the sound of Jye's voice, she found him standing in the doorway of the bedroom wearing nothing more than a resort towel draped around his hips. Flinging her arms across the doorway, as much to support her weakened knees as to block the entrance of the woman trying to get past her, Stephanie opened her mouth, only to find no words would come out.

'It's me, Jye!' Tory answered, shoving her way past Stephanie into the cabin. 'I— Oh!'

That even loose 'n' lusty Tory was left speechless by the blatant display of masculinity made Stephanie feel somewhat less gauche, and rallied her from her stupor.

'Jye, darling, Lady Mulligan wants to speak with you. Can you spare her a minute?'

'Sure thing. Morning, Tory!' Jye produced a killer smile. 'I won't be long. You and Steff chat while I throw something on.'

Once the source of her distraction had departed, Stephanie once again was able to resume her role. Graciously she waved the other woman towards a chair. 'Sorry about that, Lady Mulligan,' she said. 'You got us at a bad time.'

'Really?' A perfectly arched eyebrow rose in scepticism. 'I've been knocking for ages.'

'Oh… Guess we weren't really listening for the door. Perhaps you should've called—' Theatrically she smacked a hand against her forehead, as if struck by a second thought. 'Oh, that's right! Jye probably took the phone off the hook…' Assuming a sheepish expression, she let her words die to a shrug.

A sly smile edged across Tory's mouth. '*Still* does that, does he?'

*Bitch!* Stephanie thought, even as she cursed herself for surrendering to overkill with the bit about the phone.

'Okay, I'm decent!'

Jye's quick re-entrance in khaki beach shorts and T-shirt had Stephanie on the verge of a relieved sigh; that was until he grabbed her waist and pulled her against him to drop a quick kiss on her lips.

'I meant what I said about resting today,' he told her, his hand splaying over her hip as he spoke. 'Last night only proves what I've been saying about you overdoing it.'

'*Jye,*' she said, stilling his hand with her own and hoping she sounded lovingly exasperated rather than like the potential cardiac victim her heart-rate suggested. 'I'm…eh, fine. Truly, I feel wonderful.'

His dark eyes sparked with amusement. 'You do.'

She swallowed hard. Had she only imagined his response as a statement rather than a question? He made no attempt to release his hold on her, and the heat of his hands was radiating through the shirt to singe every cell of her body. Short of pulling away and making a scene, Stephanie could do nothing else except smile up at him and murmur yet another assurance that she was fine.

'I still think she's a tad pale, don't you, Tory?'

Tory's grunted response was at best non-committal, but Jye acted as if it had been an endorsement of his pseudo-concern.

'Sounds like it's two against one, sweetheart,' he said, giving Stephanie such a genuine look of affection she decided he not only had the physical attributes of a Hollywood idol, but the talent as well.

'So, Tory,' he said. 'What was it you wanted to see me about?'

'Unfortunately Frank's had something urgent come up, and isn't going to be able to meet with you today as planned…'

Stephanie had heard a hangover called 'bad', 'severe', even 'terminal', but never *urgent*.

'But rather than have you inconvenienced by a wasted day,' Tory continued, making a production out of crossing one long bare leg over the other, as if fearful her billboard-sized advertisement for plastic surgery might quite literally put the rest of her assets in the shade, 'he's suggested I fill in for him and show you some of the things that make the Illusion Island Resort so unique.'

*Starting with your bedroom, I'll bet!* Stephanie thought. Though she'd never previously held a firm opinion one way or the other on the subject of titles being outmoded in this day and age, having met Lady Mulligan, she was now convinced the whole procedure was in desperate need of some quality control checks.

'Well, the thing is, Tory,' Jye said smoothly, 'I was about to call Sir Frank and cancel out today myself. I don't like leaving Steff alone when she's not well.'

The other woman laughed. 'But Jye, she's just admitted she's perfectly fine now. And I'm sure your wife is as anxious as the rest of us to have the Porter Resort Corporation and Illusions come to a mutually beneficial agreement as quickly as possible. Aren't you, Stephanie, dear?'

It was a good thing she hadn't eaten, she decided, because as skittish as Jye was making her stomach, Tory's nauseatingly sweet smile would have made her empty it on the spot!

'Lady Mulligan's right, Jye. I'm perfectly well enough to join you on a tour of the island.'

'No!' Tory burst out vehemently, before modifying her tone. 'That is, it'd probably be best if you didn't.' Sickening smile number two was produced. 'We wouldn't want the heat and sun to cause a relapse in your health.'

'I agree with you, Tory,' Jye said. The comment earned him a pleased smile from one woman, while the one tucked beneath his arm stiffened and delivered a furtive, wicked pinch to his arm. Giving the platinum pincher a discreet pat to her cute little butt, he smiled into her outraged eyes.

'Now, darling, don't look like that. You really *shouldn't* be doing anything more than resting today…' He fought laughter as outrage was superseded by a promise of murder, then qualified his words by adding, '*And I intend to stay right here and make sure you don't.*' Instantly her body relaxed against his, and his amusement switched to something else.

'Thanks anyway, Tory, but I'll have to turn down your offer. Tell Sir Frank to call me later, and we'll set something up for tomorrow.'

The other woman's overly made-up face was tight with annoyance. 'Very well! But in that case, Jye, may I suggest *you leave your phone on the hook so he can reach you!*'

'What the devil did she mean by that?' Jye asked as he turned back from closing the door.

That he was completely bamboozled by the other woman's exit line sent Stephanie's heart soaring, but she substituted the urge to giggle with a shrug.

'By the way,' Jye said, when she started to turn away from an appraisal that was making her feel extremely self-conscious. 'I've come up with a couple of ideas on how we can deal with the problem of Carey.'

'Right now I'd rather you come up with some coffee, while I get dressed. There's an electric jug and complimentary tea and coffee in the kitchen.'

'What's the rush?'

'Severe caffeine withdrawal,' she tossed over her shoulder *en route* to the bathroom.

'I meant…what's the rush to get dressed? Personally, I happen to think you look terrific wearing my favourite shirt…'

Jye's voice sounded deep, seductive and serious. It seemed to reach down deep inside her and stroke at everything that made her female. *Which was absolutely ludicrous!* she told herself. All he was doing was engaging in his usual light-hearted teasing, and instead of stupidly imagining it was anything more, she should fire back the witty retort he was no doubt expecting. Except she couldn't think of anything remotely witty, and even if she had it would have been impossible to verbalise; her tongue was stuck to the roof of her mouth, her pulse was in overdrive and her lungs completely stalled.

She made her way towards the bathroom by continuing to put one shaky leg in front of the other. Never had she been so incredibly aware of a man in her life. She could literally *feel* his gaze on her back. It took all her will-power to ignore the little voice in her head urging her to *turn around and see what his face is saying*. Once ensconced in the tiled seclusion of the small room, she sagged against the closed door and sank to the cool tile floor.

Dragging in long, deep breaths, she worked at reining in her over the top emotions and getting some sort of grip on this sudden physical awareness she'd started to feel for Jye. *Jye*, for God's sake!

Forget the fact she'd known him all her life and that he was nothing like the men she'd previously been attracted to; *she* didn't come within a bull's roar of being *his* type! Sure, she could scratch up glamour and sophistication for the sake of business, but basically she was domestic cask wine in a plastic tumbler, when Jye's taste ran to exotic champagne in well-curved crystal.

What really bothered her, though, wasn't that she was afraid she *couldn't* compete for his attention, but the fact that she *wanted* to! What was more, she thought ruefully, she could sit here practising regulated breathing techniques for the next hour and it wasn't going to do any flipping good! The scent of his aftershave hanging in the small room was as hauntingly arousing as the lingering traces of his maleness clinging to the fabric against her bare skin. Glancing down at what she affectionately called her breasts, and their now rigidly aroused tips, she groaned.

As if being confronted by Jye's raw male sexuality wasn't enough for her to have to contend with, suddenly her own previously well-submerged sensuality was demanding notice too!

# CHAPTER SEVEN

BY JYE'S calculations it was seventeen minutes before Stephanie joined him on the patio. More than enough time for her to have blowdried her hair into one of those fashionably sophisticated styles she invariably wore into the office each morning but which rarely lasted beyond lunchtime; yet when she appeared her silver-blonde hair was still wet enough to hold the tell-tale ridges of the comb that had swept it back from her face.

Her face was still free of make-up and, strangely, seeing her virtually fresh from the shower struck him as being almost as arousing as seeing her in his shirt had been. Of course after the tantalising expanse of leg the shirt had displayed the ankle-length yellow and orange dress she wore was something of a let-down; although on the other end of things it *was* strapless and showed off more of her long, elegant neck and smooth amber-tinted shoulders.

Appreciative as he was, however, of the picture she made stretched out in the lounger beside him, he was unable to prevent a gag of disgust when she picked up her now cold coffee and started to drink it.

'There's a microwave inside, you know.'

'Nah, this is fine. It's the content not the temperature I need. I'll have a hot cup of the percolated stuff when we go up for breakfast.'

'We aren't going up for breakfast,' he told her. 'We can't risk running into Carey.'

She stared at him. 'Call me unprofessional, Jye, but I'm not starving myself to death in the interests of Porter's. *That* is taking things too far!'

He laughed. 'You draw the line of dedication to the company at marrying me, uh?'

'Huh! If I'd actually *known* what I was getting into coming here, I'd have drawn it a lot closer to home—*like at my office door*,' she said fervently.

'Relax. I'm not asking you to lay down your life for the company… Not today at any rate.'

'Gee, thanks, but with Tory gunning for me that's hardly reassuring.'

He smiled. 'Remember how Sir Frank magnanimously granted us round-the-clock room service?' At her nod he continued. 'Well, we're going to avail ourselves of the offer and avoid the dining room and the main resort in general for a couple of days. It mightn't stop Tory dropping by unexpectedly, but it should solve the problem of Carey.'

At her questioningly raised arched eyebrow he explained. 'I know for a fact he's due back in the office in three days' time. Considering how much trouble he went to to get this promotion, he's not going to put it at risk by starting out tardy.'

'You're wrong, Jye.'

'You think he will risk—'

She shook her head. 'No, no. I mean you're wrong about his vacation time. His secretary told me he wasn't due back for two weeks.'

Jye frowned. 'When did she tell you that?'

'The day after I got back. The day before I asked you to…eh—'

'Yeah, I know what you asked!' he cut in tersely. He didn't need reminders of how far she'd been prepared to go for Carey. 'The thing is, when I called past Carey's office that day, not realising he was *on his honeymoon*,' he said deliberately, 'I was told he was only going to be away for a week. Which would mean he's got to be out of here in three days at the max.'

'You might've misunderstood.'

'The same could be said of you.'

She shrugged and stared down into her coffee. 'I guess it's possible. I was pretty emotional.'

Jye saw no point in admitting that he'd been in a mood to break heads himself after leaving her in his office, and had made a beeline to the design floor. In hindsight it was probably a damn good thing Carey hadn't been there. Now all he had to hope was that her claim last night of concern that Carey's presence on the island would jeopardise their sham marriage was the sole reason she'd been so upset at seeing him again. Although judging by her sad, wistful expression, it was probably a faint hope.

'Jye,' she said, her head downcast. 'How far would you go for the sake of ambition?'

Gritting his teeth, he kept his curses silent, struggling between the impulse to just get up and walk away or to tell her all over again why Brad Carey wasn't worthy of her.

'Well?' she prodded.

'If you mean would I get married to get ahead—'

'No,' she said quickly. 'I…I mean would you consider using your kids as collateral, the way everyone thinks our parents did?'

The sad uncertainty in her face almost broke his heart. The circumstances of how they'd both come to be raised by Duncan Porter, millionaire bachelor, was the last thing he'd been expecting her to bring up. Still, recalling her reaction at dinner to the mention of her father, the query hadn't really come from left field.

'I wondered what effect Mulligan's comments last night were having on you,' he mused aloud.

When no response was forthcoming he cast her a furtive look, trying to gauge what she might be thinking; her expression was pensive and unrevealing as she studied the contents of her coffee cup.

'We've never talked about our parents before.' He kept his comment deliberately bland; she could either pick up on it or ignore it. It was several moments before she answered.

'To be honest, as horrible as it might sound…I rarely think about them.' Her mouth pulled into a tight smile. 'I used to, but I stopped 'cause it made me feel guilty.'

'Guilty? How?'

'I've two albums full of photographs of them and me

when I was little. I used to look at them every day and wish they were alive so I could have a real family.' She shrugged. 'Then, when I was about twelve or so, it started bothering me that I was being disloyal to Duncan. You see, it never occurred to me my parents had asked Duncan to be my godfather as a career move. Not until I overheard some executives talking about it at one of the Australia Day barbecues out at the house.'

'How old were you when that happened?'

She frowned. 'I dunno…eleven or twelve. I asked Mrs Clarence if it was true…'

'And what did Fearsome Flo say?' he asked wryly, glad of the light-hearted chuckle Steff emitted at his use of the old nickname. Flo Clarence had been the housekeeper-cum-nanny Duncan had hired when the two of them had first moved in with him. The brisk but kind woman had retired eight years ago, when Steff had completed high school, but she'd continued to maintain contact with both her former charges. Jye could practically set his clock by her regular Tuesday night phone calls.

'Oh, she just gave me one of her *well-that's-a-dang-fool-question* looks and said if I was happy living with Duncan then how I came to be there shouldn't be an issue.'

Jye grinned. It was a typically Flo response.

'After that, I just let the gossip slide by me. But you know, Jye,' she said, 'if I could have just one wish now, it wouldn't be that my parents hadn't died, but to *know* with absolute certainty they really loved me. That they didn't just make Duncan my godfather so Dad could get in his good books. Duncan deserves better than that.'

She gave a self-conscious shrug. 'Your turn. You ever wonder about how your parents felt?'

'No.'

The curt response and the shuttered look on his face said he'd answered her question and he wasn't going to offer anything more. She was about to change the subject when he gave a self-deprecating laugh.

'What the hell!' he said. 'If I'm going to compare scars with anyone, it might as well be you.'

Since it was obvious he was less than enthusiastic about discussing his parents, Stephanie knew the polite thing to do would be to tell him it wasn't necessary. But she kept her mouth shut, because suddenly she craved to know all she could about Jye. About his early childhood.

'All my grandparents were long dead before I was born,' he started. 'My mother was an only child and my father only had a younger sister, whom we rarely saw since she and Dad clashed. Gemma lived on a commune up in northern New South Wales, and was as much a flower-child and free spirit as my old man was a corporate shark and social climber.

'For some reason, though, she came to visit us when I was about eight years old. To me, a prep school student from the upper middle classes, Clover—that's what she called herself,' he explained, 'couldn't have been more of an alien if she'd been green and had antennae coming out of her head.'

There was an edge of hesitancy in Jye' s voice that suggested he was examining memories that had faded from lack of use. Like peering at an old photograph you remembered taking, but could no longer understand why you had, or why you'd kept it.

'On this particular visit Clover was going through a stage where she was obsessed with death and family. Although I'm not sure which one got top billing,' he said dryly. 'And, of course, reincarnation. She went on and on about reincarnation. Ticked the old man off something fierce, it did, but you know,' he said, 'for months after her visit I couldn't walk past a stray dog or cat without stopping and wondering who it had been in its past life...' He laughed, this time with what sounded like genuine amusement and fondness, before abruptly stopping.

'Anyway,' he continued, his expression again impassive, 'one night we were all sitting down to dinner when Clover announced my parents should be fully prepared for their deaths, that they should make out wills ensuring my future by naming her my guardian in the event of them dying together. Well, when my parents stopped laughing and picked themselves up off the floor, they blithely told her if they so much as named *her* guardian of a philodendron their accountant would have them committed long before they had to worry about their next incarnation.

'They softened the blow by reassuring her they had, however, made wills. To paraphrase my mother, they'd *not only ensured my well-being when they moved on to the next life, but ensured their future in this one by naming Duncan my guardian.*'

Hard black eyes fixed on her. 'So you see, Steff, unlike you I was spared the anguish of wondering about my parents' motivation in naming Duncan as my guardian.'

It was impossible to miss the harshness in Jye's tone, and Stephanie didn't know how to respond to it.

After a silence that threatened to stretch for ever it was Jye who spoke. 'I was ten when the accident happened. Old enough to know my parents weren't perfect, or even like those of my classmates. Mum didn't volunteer for canteen duty at school, and my father probably thought a school working bee was some sort of insect.

'As an adult I can look back and acknowledge that they didn't have a happy marriage, but I can't claim they stayed together out of anything as noble as giving me a stable upbringing. It was my father's career ambitions and financial success that kept them together. Nothing else. In a way their dying together at a Porter's function was a bizarre but fitting way for them to go. Ironically, the best thing they probably ever did for me was to use me as a means of getting closer to Duncan, because he's been more a parent to me than either of them were ever capable of being.'

He turned his head and trapped Stephanie's gaze in his. 'The stories that our fathers were always competing against each other have always seemed entirely plausible to me, simply because I know exactly the type of man my father was. I didn't know yours, so I can't guess at *his* motives;

maybe he didn't want mine to "have an edge" over him; maybe making Duncan your godfather stemmed from some entirely sincere reason. I don't know. But I *do* know we've both been damn lucky to have had Duncan, Steff,' he told her.

Stephanie simply smiled. No verbal response was necessary.

'The answer to your original question—which,' Jye went on, 'is purely hypothetical, since I've no intention of ever having children, is *no*. I wouldn't use my kids as collateral to further my career. Any more than I'd enter into a marriage of convenience to get a promotion. And that...' he grinned '...forces me to point out that if Brad Carey had been of a similar mind we wouldn't be in our current predicament.'

Relieved that the bitterness in his voice had evaporated, she was more than willing to avoid further probing of his past and return the focus to their present problems.

'Even if you're right and I'm wrong about when Brad's due back in Sydney,' she said, 'how can you avoid the resort? Mulligan's going to insist on meeting you there for the home turf advantage.'

The face Jye pulled made him look endearingly boyish. 'That's the part of my plan I'm still fine-tuning. Just our rotten luck that Carey didn't avail himself of the staff discount plan and go to one of Porter's resorts.'

'Why don't we just call Duncan and have him check the leave roster to confirm how long Brad's likely to be here?' she suggested.

'The only phones linked to the mainland are in Mulligan's penthouse and the main office of the resort. I can't take the risk of being overheard trying to explain to Duncan why I want to know.'

'We could always use the mobile.'

'I tried that when I called to get you over here. Trust me, it was pretty much a lost cause from the start.'

'Well, thanks very mu—'

'*The call itself, Steff!*' he hastily clarified. 'The line kept dropping out every few seconds; the only thing constant was the static. We were lucky if we managed to make out every fifth word the other said.'

'It can't have been that bad. I'm here, aren't I?'

He looked at her for a long time before his mouth twitched. 'Yeah... But I'm chalking that up to this year's supply of my good luck.'

Feeling ridiculously self-conscious, she forced a disbelieving laugh.

'I'm being serious, Steff.'

Her pulse burst into an erratic jig and she lifted her empty coffee cup and pretended to drink from it, just to break eye contact without appearing too obvious. Frantically she searched her mind for something impersonal but relevant to say to fill the silence. Finding nothing, she began groping for a plausible excuse for getting up and leaving. It came to her in the ignominious form of a tummy rumble.

'Don't say a word,' she warned as Jye raised an amused eyebrow.

'Hey... *I* didn't make a sound.'

'I'm going to order breakfast.' She stood up. 'Anything special you'd like?'

'Well, that depends Stephanie,' he drawled, making a slow, *very slow* appraisal of her body before bringing his eyes back to her face. 'Are you asking specifically about breakfast, or is that a...general enquiry?'

'B-b-breakfast!' she stammered, hoping her face wasn't as red as it felt; although judging by his grin it probably was. Why was it her mind had suddenly started turning every innocent remark he made into a sexual innuendo? For heaven's sake, by 'general enquiry' he'd probably meant was she offering to get him the morning paper or... or...something.

Realising she'd not heard a word of what he'd just said, she had to ask him to repeat it.

'I said, since you're only offering to *fix me up* with

breakfast, I'll have to settle for something boring, like OJ, fruit, coffee and bacon and eggs.'

His chuckle followed her all the walk back into the cabin…the seductive tone of his initial response to her went through her head for much, much longer.

Jye set aside the purchase proposal he'd been attempting to study when he heard a knock on the cabin door and Steff hurrying to open it. He entered the cabin just as she wheeled a covered stainless steel traymobile towards the kitchenette.

'And not a moment too soon,' he said, sliding the lid back. 'I'm starving! *What the—?*' He broke off in disgust and looked at the broadly grinning blonde, who as yet hadn't seen the contents of the tray.

'Don't get too excited,' he warned her. 'Everything's bloody raw!'

'I know,' she stated, still beaming. 'That's how I asked for it.'

'Excuse me?'

'When I ordered they asked if I wanted it cooked or uncooked. I said—'

'*I can guess what you said, Steff.* What I want to know is why?'

'So I can cook it for us myself, of course.'

'Oh, God.' It was a genuine prayer for divine intervention. To have to face one of Steff's culinary catastrophes as well as sleep deprivation was too cruel a fate for any man.

'At first I couldn't work out why the kitchenette was complete,' she prattled on. 'But apparently Sir Frank has this really fabulous idea for people who see cooking as a recreational activity and who, like me, would like to be able to cook while they're here.'

He had no doubt Steff would *like* to be able to cook *anywhere*; the fact was, she couldn't! And while cooking might be a recreational activity for some people, Jye, and probably all foreign governments, would have classified her efforts as experimenting with chemical warfare.

'Steff, I think it'd be better if we ordered our meals fully prepared.'

'Why?'

'Eh...because it'll be much less hassle. Less time-consuming,' he said, realising he'd come up with a trump argument. 'This place doesn't have a dishwasher.'

'Not a problem. Everything gets sent back to the resort kitchen for that; after all, *nobody* considers washing dishes a recreational activity.'

*Wonderful!* he thought. Now what subtle excuse could he come up with?

'Steff, honey...it's still a lot of work for you. I really hate the thought of you slaving over a hot st—'

'Oh, knock it off, Jye!'' she burst in disgust. 'I'm not stupid. It's because you think I can't cook, isn't it?' she demanded. 'Go on, be honest! That's it, isn't it?'

She wanted honesty? Fine! The gloves were off. He'd had enough of acting as if her cute smile and sexy little body were reason enough for him to pander to her.

'No,' he said. 'It's not because I think you can't cook. It's because I *know* you can't.'

'I told you I've been taking lessons!'

'How many have you had?'

'Half a semester.'

'How many lessons, Steff?'

'Five, okay! I had five lessons before I went to Perth. And if I hadn't had to go on that dumb trip I'd be almost through my Beginners Basics stage,' she told him. 'For your information, my instructor said I showed real promise!'

'So did my Year Eight science teacher, and I blew up half the chem lab in Year Ten!' Jye retorted. *'And that was after two years of advanced level science!'*

'Well, if you're *that* useless, stay the hell out of the kitchen! Here!' She shoved a plate filled with raw bacon, two eggs and what looked like frozen hash browns at him.

'I don't care if you eat it raw, take it up to the resort or shove it up your—'

'Oh for God's sake, Stephanie! Why do you have such a damn bee in your bonnet about cooking? It's not a crime if a woman can't cook. Why knock yourself out trying to do something you're not cut out for? What's this obsession you've got with proving you can cook? You think being able to whip up a soufflé is going to make you more feminine or attractive than a woman who can't—'

'You leave my femininity alone! For your information, I'm more than happy with it! When I'm not I'll be studying breast implant procedures, not cookbooks!'

*'You'll what?'*

'And furthermore,' she said, dragging Jye beyond his dumbfounded reaction to her last statement by waving a fork in his face, 'I'm not trying to *prove* anything to anyone! Least of all *you*, Jye Fox!

Self-preservation had him taking a quick backward step as she jabbed the pronged weapon perilously close to his throat.

'I enjoy cooking! It relaxes me and makes me feel creative…'

Figuring if she got any more *relaxed* or *creative* over breakfast he'd be the first thing getting carved up, Jye remained mute.

'And one day I'm going to be so damn good I'm going to open my own restaurant! And when I do, Jye Fox,' she said, her eyes narrowing with steely conviction, 'I'm going to get the biggest, meanest bouncer I can find to man the door and give him instructions not to let you in!'

He couldn't stop his mouth from twitching at the irony of it all. She mightn't be able to boil water, but with her beautiful little mouth going a million miles an hour as she roared at him, her face flushed with murderous intent, she sure got his blood bubbling. In the last twenty-four hours their relationship had really heated up.

'What's so funny?' she demanded.

For a moment he seriously considered telling her exactly

what he'd been thinking, but decided she was too ticked off to run the risk. Instead he smiled, opting to tease her back into a good mood. 'A restaurant, huh? Well, yeah, I suppose it's possible...'

Her expression immediately lightened. 'You do?'

'Mmm. Of course, you want to hope the bouncer works cheap...' He winked at her. ''Cause, honey, with your reputation the insurance premiums are going to really rough up your profit margin!'

As anger and hurt vied for the title of her most dominant emotion, Stephanie reacted to both by ramming the trolley at Jye and bolting out of the front door while he was still hopping around clutching his leg and cursing.

For a moment there she'd thought he was going to say something encouraging. Something like 'I suppose it's possible...with hard work and determination'. But oh, no! He had to keep shooting her down in flames. Like he was an expert on cooking! He probably hadn't walked into a kitchen since he'd discovered they didn't have beds!

Okay, so her owning a restaurant might possibly seem a little far-fetched now, but that didn't mean it was an impossible goal! Just because a woman wasn't born being able to cook, it didn't mean she couldn't learn. She hadn't been born able to talk, or walk or...or sail, and look how good she'd become at all of them! Of course, no one had told her she couldn't, whereas everybody was ready to openly discourage her attempts at cooking! Jye had been teasing her about her cooking ever since that first dinner she'd cooked, after Mrs Clarence had retired, when she'd accidentally roasted a chicken with the plastic bag full of giblets still inside it. Well, she was fed up with his stirring! And with him!

With no thought to, or knowledge of, where the shaded path to her right would take her, Stephanie followed it, too het up to view the exotic tropical plants and towering trees on either side of it as anything but a hiding place if Jye decided to pursue her. But when she carelessly stomped her bare foot down on a sharp twig she swore softly, and took a longer look at the island's thick vegetation, wondering if she shouldn't revise her plan. Which would be worse? Confronting a mean, agile snake with a venomous bite or confronting Jye? She glanced nervously over her shoulder, then laughed. 'Ha! Like there's a noticeable difference!'

Taking great pleasure in mentally comparing Jye Fox's *poison*ality with that of the world's most deadly reptiles, she didn't notice the ever-increasing sunlight until she found herself blinking against its blinding brightness as the tropical forest ended. Automatically she raised her hand to shade her eyes as she perused a scene of such sheer beauty and tranquillity it sucked a good portion of the tension she'd been cultivating from her body.

Her toes were touching the outer rim of a horseshoe of pearl-white sand, the inner curve lapped by water so sparkling clear it looked like liquid aquamarine. Having read the activities brochure at the cabin, and in the obvious absence of any 'friendly waves to frolic in', she surmised she was looking at Illusion Inlet and not Jewel Beach, which had been described as the island's 'premier beach playground'. But to her way of thinking the beach would really have to be something special to outshine this.

'Pretty spectacular, huh?'

Surprise caused her to jump. The fact Jye had frightened the life out of her made her almost as furious as the fact he had the nerve to be smiling.

'It was until you turned up,' she said, quickly averting her eyes.

'Look, I'm sorry.'

'Actions speak louder than words, so prove it and get lost.'

'Steff…'

A fountain of sparks burst through her blood as his hands settled on her bare shoulders. His thumbs began idly grazing her back as his fingers rested against the ridge of her clavicle.

'Listen a minute…'

Listen? Her heart was pounding loud enough to drown

out a heavy metal concert. As if that wasn't enough, her treacherous little hormones had shifted into party mode and were tempting her to lean back against him. She stiffened her spine in the hope he'd release her. He didn't. And she was too stupidly weak to step away.

'I didn't mean to upset you. Truly. I thought you were kidding about the restaurant; you've never mentioned it before.'

'I...I don't talk about it because I prefer not to invite ridicule.'

Jye groaned inwardly. She sounded only one breath away from crying, the tightness of her voice matching the rigid brace of her shoulders. If he'd ever felt a bigger heel, he couldn't remember when.

'Apart from you,' she continued, 'I...I've never mentioned it to anyone. But don't worry, I won't make the mistake of publicly voicing my dreams again. I wouldn't even have told you if you hadn't got me so angry.'

Her shoulders sank on a shakily expelled breath. 'You reacted like me wanting to cook breakfast was the crime of the century. Like I was going to deliberately poison you or something.'

'Honey...I'm sorry. The truth is...it wasn't so much the idea of your cooking that set me off this morning. It's just—'

*Just what, you turkey?* his brain taunted. *Just that you've suddenly realised even though she's flat out making an edible peanut butter sandwich, you'd happily eat glass to get her into your bed?*

*Right, tell her that! She should be real responsive to that explanation right now!*

'Just what, Jye?' she asked stiffly.

'Just this whole crazy situation,' he improvised, turning her to face him. Again her natural beauty gave him pause. 'I truly am sorry for hurting you, Steff. And if—'

Poleaxed didn't come close to describing his reaction when with lightning swiftness she took a two-fisted hold of his shirt and reduced the foot and a half of space between them to nothing. Her eyes were big saucers as she raised them to him, and simultaneously he experienced both alarm and arousal.

'Steff, wh—'

'Shh!' she hissed. 'That crazy situation you were talking about is about to peak; *Brad's coming down the path behind you.*'

Clamping down on the instinctive urge to turn around, Jye swore under his breath. 'How far away is he?'

'Sixty feet. And closing!' Her tone and face were urgent. 'If we move it we can probably disappear on the beach.' Grasping his forearm, she turned in that direction. 'C'mon, let's go!'

'No!' Jye checked her movement. 'He'll notice us if we run.'

'And he'll get a positive ID if we don't!' Stephanie gave his arm another solid tug. Again his resistance frustrated her, and she shot him an impatient glare.

'Steff, this is the only path off the beach. If he plants himself here, we're stuck till he leaves. It could be hours.'

'So we'll risk a case of sunburn!' she muttered, beginning to think the only way to move Jye was to actually call out to Brad and get him to grab his other arm.

'Jye, *come on*!' Though she tugged his arm with all her might it was a futile effort against his superior strength, which was suddenly hauling *her* in the opposite direction to the treed area. *Towards the ever-advancing Brad.*

'*Jye!*' she whispered frantically as he pressed her against a tree Brad would be passing within seconds. '*What are you doing?*'

'Kissing you. Consider yourself warned…'

# CHAPTER EIGHT

STEPHANIE fought to keep her eyes open. If she closed them the burst of unparalleled joy she was feeling at Jye's announcement would instantly evaporate. But her will-power was no match for the hypnotic effect of the male body pressing against hers, nor the will-sapping sensations of Jye's mouth and tongue moving across her own. Yet when her lids inevitably did close Stephanie discovered the surrender in no way diminished the awareness swimming through her; instead it seemed to magnify it out of all proportion, distorting logic until reality became the surreal...

Jye's scent replaced the fresh salt air she'd previously been inhaling, and the ocean which moments ago had lapped silently at the sand became her blood, crashing through her veins like storm-whipped surf. It was a struggle to breathe; excitement, confusion and panic flailed wildly and futilely within her until she was so physically exhausted her legs started to tremble weakly. Her heart, though, was pumping stronger and faster than it ever had before.

She might have been on dry land, but Stephanie knew she was drowning; irrefutably going down for the third time. Yet in that instant she also knew that if her life was going to flash before her eyes, she wanted this man to be the last image she saw, and pressing closer to him was the most fundamental of actions.

The grateful moan which met her ears as she clasped his neck and brought her tongue against his might just as possibly have come from Jye as from her, but it reverberated through her entire body. A body more achingly aware of itself than it had ever been as it was assailed by sensations and emotions so alien to its owner they frightened her... And seduced her. Seduced her so beautifully she wanted to

101

know more about them, became desperate to learn *everything* about them so she might recognise them again.

So she clung tighter to their strong male source, surrendering herself deeper into his magic, and found these strange new sensations continued to grow and multiply until she was sure she could reach and touch them. But they proved frustratingly elusive, and each time she thought she could identify one another intruded to distract and blur her brain even more. Again and again it happened...until she was giddy...until she felt her bones would melt and—

Dimly she heard someone call her name, and in that fleeting moment of distraction the sensations began to recede. To ebb away, gently...softly...quietly...until only one remained, its solitary survival standing as a testament to its supremacy.

*Love.*

In the past she and this emotion had been acquaintances, but now Stephanie no longer recognised it merely by name. Now she recognised it with her heart. *Felt* it there and knew it was entrenched so firmly it would never leave. Amazed and stunned by the realisation, she slowly opened her eyes, blinking rapidly as blinding sunlight welcomed her back to the reality of Illusion Island.

But reality didn't change a thing... She, Stephanie Elizabeth Bernadette Worthington, was *in love* with Jye Fox.

'Maybe I was the one who should've been warned.'

Jye's muttered remark barely registered in her bemused brain, but the wary expression on his face as he glanced towards the beach all too quickly reminded Stephanie that the motivation behind him kissing her hadn't sprung from his heart. He'd kissed her only to avoid them being recognised by the man who could blow their charade. Jye, as always, was being pragmatic not romantic.

'Is he...?' Hearing the breathless quality in her words, Stephanie paused to suck in more air. 'Is he gone?'

'Yeah...they're gone.'

The coal-black eyes switched back to study her, as if

trying to probe her deepest secrets. The alarming notion had her quickly pushing away from the tree and trying to imitate normality. 'Good. Then let's get out of here before he decides to come back.'

'You weren't listening, Steff.' Jye's tone was crisp. 'I said, *they're* gone...Karrie was with him.'

Jye noted surprise was the first emotion to register in Steff's face at his words, closely followed by confusion and, as he'd feared, disbelief and denial.

'I didn't see anyone with him.' She frowned at him. 'Are you sure it was Karrie?'

An overwhelming desire to spare her feelings momentarily tempted him to say he wasn't. Then the memories of how she'd tasted and felt in his arms erupted in his head, and pure selfishness had him embracing the adage about being cruel to be kind. Stephanie *would* get over this thing she had for Carey, because he was going to help her. Damn it! *Make her.*

'It was Karrie Dent, all right. She was a few seconds behind Carey, walking with an elderly woman and admiring the vegetation.'

Stephanie could only stare at him. While he'd had her totally and mindlessly enmeshed in an earth—no, *life*-shattering kiss, he'd been composed enough to simultaneously execute a surveillance that would have done James Bond proud! Sheesh! Either he could also balance *War and Peace* on his knees and read it while reverse parking, or her kissing techniques made her a cordon bleu chef! As insults went, Jye's indifference was a most crippling one, but pride demanded she had to let it slide by her. Her pride had a lot to answer for, but not nearly as much as her *stupid, indiscriminate heart*!

Stephanie was so remote and broodingly silent all the way back to the cabin that Jye wanted to shake her. Well, maybe not *shake* her, but definitely shake her up. The kiss they'd shared had come close to blowing the top of his head off, and *still* had his blood circulating at the speed of light. It had impacted on him so hard and fast he'd had to summon every ounce of will-power he possessed to end it, or he'd have had her naked on the ground before she knew what had hit her. And as responsive as Steff might've seemed at the time—*and, man, had she felt responsive*—her reaction to learning Carey's wife definitely *was* on the island had thrown ice water on any egotistical hopes Jye might have had that her interest in the jerk could be diverted.

Damn it! He wanted to be furious with her, but her downcast head and withdrawn manner as they walked up the path to the cabin had him scrambling for a way to lift her spirits instead.

Jye bravely reloaded his fork, returned it to his mouth and bit down. While swallowing without chewing had at first seemed the best way to minimise damage to his taste buds, just two mouthfuls had shown him the practice could have dangerous side effects. He wasn't sure if Steff had confused the recipes for boiled and fried eggs, or if she routinely cooked both with their shells, but these were the *crunchiest* eggs ever to pass his lips.

'I know you said you liked your bacon crispy,' she said, her own plate already half empty. 'But I was afraid I'd burn it if I left it on much longer. I can put it back on, if you want?'

'Er…no. No. This is…is fine.'

She looked so damned pleased with herself that Jye patted himself on the back for having the forethought to shove the food in the bar fridge before racing after her earlier. So what if he'd had to hedge and fib to get her to overlook his insults of a couple of hours ago? Sitting across from her now cheerful smile convinced him the end result justified the means; the look of unabashed delight that lit up her eyes every time he refilled his fork made him decide martyrdom had an up side. Hell! At this rate he'd not only eat every morsel of the half-raw bacon floating in fat, the eggs that crunched like gravel and the semi-frozen hash browns, but he'd ask for seconds!

*And pray to God there weren't any!*

'I have improved, don't you think, Jye?'

To avoid an outright lie, he shoved more food into his mouth and gave an indistinct mumble.

'If that's not enough for you, there are some Pop Tarts. Want me to toast one for you?'

'*God, no!* Er...I mean, thanks anyway, but this is plenty for now.'

Perfect white teeth, which his tongue *knew* were as smooth as they looked, flashed at him from behind a brilliant smile a split second before they bit into a piece of blackened toast. Jye fought back a moan as razor-sharp pain stabbed him in the chest. At another time he'd have taken one look at what he was shovelling into his mouth and blamed indigestion, except the symptoms weren't quite right. To the best of his recall indigestion had never left him with a hard-on before. Oh, Lord, he groaned inwardly, shifting in his chair, when a man started aspiring to be a bit of charred bread, he was in *serious* trouble!

*She was in serious trouble.*

Falling in love with a confirmed bachelor was a big mistake. When the bachelor in question was Jye Fox it magnified it into a *humongous* mistake that bordered on insanity. It also denied her even the option of saying, *Aw, what the hell! I'll have a wild fling and make a few memories!*

Not that she'd ever engaged in a fling, wild or otherwise, but hypothetically, were she to decide to take the chance on one, it couldn't be with Jye Fox. No, that *would* definitely be lunacy. For one thing ending an affair with Jye would create a difficult, awkward and potentially complicated situation for a whole host of people, not the least Duncan. Then again, *starting* an affair with Jye would create an even more difficult, awkward and potentially complicated situation—not least for *her* because Jye merely regarded her as, quote, 'someone who could think on her feet.'

'But damn it,' she muttered, fighting the waterbed to sit up. 'I want him to want me *mindless and flat on my back!*'

Hearing the truth, aloud and in her own voice, startled her. *When had she come to that decision?* More importantly why, when until twenty-four hours ago she'd scarcely been *aware* of having any sexual interest in Jye, didn't she feel even faintly shy and inhibited at the thought of making love to him?

*Because you've fallen in love with him, you idiot!* Her common sense berated.

With a heartfelt groan, she swung her feet to the floor and, elbows on knees, dropped her head in her hands.

It was nearly one in the morning, and here she was too upset and churned up to even cry herself to sleep, which in itself was significant, since she'd done exactly that over every other guy she'd fallen for since the age of fourteen. The thing was, what she felt for Jye was so much stronger and utterly unique that her emotions, her reactions, her frustrations and...well, *everything* were such that she didn't know how to deal with them. In all possible areas of comparison, Jye Fox was nothing like the men she'd previously been attracted to; nothing like the perceived image of *the* man she had always aspired to marry. Of course, as usual, what she had *thought* she wanted, *known* she needed and actually *ended up with* had meshed about as well as the late Mother Teresa, Charles Manson and the Easter Bunny!

The ridge of her mother's wedding ring pressing against her cheek was further mocking reminder of the irony of life as she knew it.

For years she'd wanted nothing more than to fall hopelessly in love and get married. *And what did she get?* Hopeless love and a sham marriage to a man who viewed matrimony as the worst epidemic since the plague. But the *really* cruel thing about all this was discovering Jye would be good at marriage!

He was tidy, good-humoured—well, most of the time. If today was any guide he wasn't at his best before breakfast, but he'd come round once he'd eaten. He was thoughtful too… Why, when she'd announced she intended to cook dinner last night he'd nearly fallen over himself to help. She smiled, recalling how he'd got carried away and ordered *six* steaks from the hotel kitchen. Although she had to admit his inexperienced enthusiasm had turned out to be a stroke of luck when for no reason the dumb grill had gone mad and set fire to the first two steaks she'd put on! Jye, though, had had the fire out within seconds, and to be honest he wasn't as useless in the kitchen as she'd feared, even if he was pedantic about reading directions and stuff like that.

She sighed. Yes, Jye had the potential to make a terrific husband; the regrettable part was he had about as much inclination in that direction as Tory Mulligan did a Carmelite convent!

Her mind's wayward reference to the vampish brunette was another cruel reminder to Stephanie that she wasn't the type of woman Jye Fox had affairs with, and it brought her swiftly to her feet. Feeling hurt, angry and edgy enough to climb the walls, she quickly decided that if she didn't do something to break her mind of the vicious circular path it was dragging her along she was going to implode.

'Okay, Stephanie,' she said. '*Think.* What can a person do alone on a tropical island at one a.m.?'

As inspiration struck, she hurried into the bathroom, turned on the spa bath and quickly dumped two bottles of the resort's complimentary bubble bath under the jet. Now all she needed was a good book and a glass of wine. She allowed herself a satisfied smile; there was wine in the fridge, and the latest Stephen King offering in her luggage…

Jye woke to a high-pitched wail, a blood-curdling scream and…*the stench of smoke*!

Vaulting from the open sofa, he flew across the room, sparing only a quick glance towards the kitchenette as his hand threw open the door to the bedroom. His heart lurched at the sight of the empty bed.

'Steff!' His raised voice was barely audible above the squealing alarm. Without slowing, he charged to the adjoining bathroom and thrust open the door.

And there she was. Wearing an expression of wide-eyed terror…and not another blessed thing.

Jye felt as if he'd been zapped by two thousand volts. His world screeched to slow motion.

She stood knee-deep in bubbles, her short blonde bob glimmering silver in the light, the ends curling from the moisture of a necklace of foam already cascading from her shoulders down over firm, high breasts, a flat, taut stomach and subtly curved hips…

Jye saw her lips form his name, but didn't hear it. It was as if all his senses save vision had deserted him. He was further transfixed when she moved, the light catching the clinging suds and making her glisten with tiny rainbows. Even after she snatched for a towel, knocking a wine bottle into the tub as she scampered out, his reactions were at best rubber-limbed. Which probably explained why, when her damp hand clutched urgently at his wrist, it barely jolted him from his daze instead of electrifying them both.

'Jye! What's that noise? Jye!'

'Smoke alarm—'

*'Oh my God, the Pop Tarts!'*

Thankfully, as Stephanie flew from the room, Jye's sanity re-entered it.

'Steff!' He darted after her, snaring a slippery arm before she made it into the smoky moonlit kitchen. *'Stay here!* I'll handle it.'

Despite the smoke, mercifully there was still no evidence of flames, and Jye determined that silencing the wall-mounted smoke detector above the sink was the first priority. Jumping onto the bench-top, he thumped the kill switch. Once… Twice… *Three bloody times!* Only the continuing wail of the alarm drowned out his cough-punctuated expletives as he wrestled with the lid of the battery housing. Finally it gave, allowing him to rip out the two energised lungs powering it and reach for the toaster.

*'Jye, be careful!'*

Stephanie heard her voice like a bellow in the sudden silence, but her wince came from seeing Jye disconnect the toaster with one vicious yank to its power cord.

*'Jye, you idiot!* Are you trying to kill yourself? You can get electrocuted doing that.'

'Faster way to go than smoke inhalation.' With the still smoking toaster held at arm's length, he motioned her towards the patio. 'Get the doors!'

Sliding the glass door fully open, she trailed him out to the patio and watched as he up-ended the toaster on the wrought-iron table. Two small black smouldering brickettes fell from it.

'Am I safe in assuming *even you* aren't going to want to eat the remains?' he asked dryly. Then he swore. 'Hell, we'd better ring the resort before—'

He was cut off by frantic calls and banging on the front door.

'Before they send out the troops,' he finished.

*'Hang on!'* he roared, his voice directed towards the front door. 'I'm coming! I'm coming!'

'No, it's okay,' Stephanie said quickly. 'I caused the fuss; I'll do the explaining.' Before she'd taken one step, a male hand clamped on her neck.

'The hell you'll go to the door like that!'

At the reminder of her towel's limitations she clutched it tighter and bolted for the bedroom.

She figured it would take a few minutes at least for Jye to reassure the staff everything was under control, which gave her exactly the same limited amount of time before he began demanding an explanation. All she had to do was compose a better one than, *Falling in love with you has turned me into a cross between an insomniac and an arsonist.* Boy, was she going to be writing a stinging letter to the makers of that dumb toaster for putting her in this position.

As her current spate of bad luck would have it, she'd barely had time to pull on a pair of knickers and reach for a T-shirt when a sharp rap on her door was followed by a rattling of the handle. Panic had her hurdling the corner of the bed to reach it before it opened, relief coursing through her as she discovered she'd automatically locked it when she came in. Right now the depressed button on that little gold knob represented the brightest point of her whole day.

'Coast's clear, Steff. You can unlock the door.'

Since even travelling through the four centimetres of timber Jye's low-pitched voice caused tingles down her naked spine, unlocking the door *was not* a smart option. To further minimise temptation, she leaned her back against it.

'Steff… C'mon, open up. I'd like to hear your explanation.'

'No.'

'*No?* You don't think I deserve an explanation as to why you wanted to barbecue me?'

'It was an accident.'

'Gosh, *that* makes me feel better.'

Clutching the T-shirt, she turned and rested her forehead against the door. 'Can't we talk about this in the morning? I'm tired, Jye.'

'Getting up in the middle of the night to take a bath and set fire to the house will do that to you every time.'

Despite herself, the amusement in his voice made her smile. 'I was having trouble sleeping. A relaxing tub seemed a good idea. I guess I forgot I put the Pop Tarts on and the toaster must've got stuck.'

'You *guess* that's what happened?' He sounded incredulous. 'You must've put away a fair bit of that wine you had in there not to have smelt the smoke, Steff. You looked pretty out of it when I found you. You're not drunk, are you?'

'Of course I'm not drunk! I only had one and a bit glasses before—'

'Settle down, honey,' he cut in to her heated denial. 'I was just asking. Although drinking in a bath when you're tired can be dangerous. If it hadn't been for the smoke detector, you might've drowned before you burned to death.'

Stephanie rolled her eyes. He sounded like a community service announcement. 'Really? Would that've made my demise a double fatality? Or merely meant I was twice as dead?'

His chuckle was warm. 'Open up and we'll discuss it.' His voice tempting. Too tempting.

'Jye, I'm tired.'

'We can both go to bed once you've told me the whole story.'

She opened her mouth to argue, then sighed. *Anything for peace!* 'Okay, for the sake of some sleep, here's a condensed version.'

'Shoot.'

'I couldn't sleep.' *Thanks to you!* she added silently. 'So I decided I'd relax in the bath with a good book and a glass of wine.'

'And the Pop Tarts,' he inserted. 'Don't want to forget them a *second* time.'

Planting her hands on her hips, she pulled a face at the door. 'I'm not up to the Pop Tarts yet! Who's telling this story? You or me?'

'Sorry. Go on,' he urged.

'*Thank you.* While the bubble bath was filling I went to get the wine, and *that's* when I saw the Pop Tarts left over from breakfast. I put them in the toaster, took the wine into the bathroom and poured a glass, and bec—' She broke off, deciding that purely in the interests of condensing the story it would be better to edit out *and because you had me so stressed out I gulped it down in one go.*

Hoping he'd missed her hesitation, she continued. 'And, er, then I got in the tub. At some point I did pour a second glass of wine,' she admitted. 'But you'll have to blame Stephen King's engrossing writing for the fact I can't give the time down to the last hundredth of a second,' she said facetiously, still irritated by his crack about her being drunk.

'Obviously I dozed off, otherwise I'd have smelt the smoke. The next thing I know I'm waking up to the wails of hell. So if I looked "out of it", as you put it, it's because I thought I'd suddenly been pitched into the middle of Chapter Fifteen as the next victim!

'And furthermore, Jye, while I know I'm responsible for all this…this *drama*, I resent your implication that it happened because I'd drunk myself into a stupor! Because I didn't.'

'No…I'm the only one in a stupor.'

At first surprise froze her. Then it had her pivoting around and gaping at the man lounging in the doorway to the bathroom.

He looked so heart-stoppingly handsome and sexy, standing with his muscled arms folded across his chest just watching her, Stephanie was certain she was only one degree from melting into the floor rug. When she'd bought him the bright yellow boxer shorts last Christmas as a joke she'd never imagined he'd even wear them, never mind wear them so well!

'My    God…You    are    so    beautiful,    Stephanie Worthington.'

It wasn't the seductive, husky awe in his statement that snapped her from her reverie, but the side effect of her stomach hitting the floor as a result of the appreciative gleam in his eyes as they washed her body. Flushing furiously, she jerked the T-shirt back up to her breasts.

'Too late, Steff…' His mouth slanted with wry amusement. 'I've already seen you wearing a lot less than knickers.'

Straightening from the wall, he began moving effortlessly and purposefully towards her.

'Eh… Jye… I, ah…er…'

Her clever attempt to counter his advance and visual caresses by stuttering, stammering and trying to back her way through the locked door didn't work. His right hand pressed against the door to the left of her head, the other easily relieving her limp hand of the T-shirt separating their bare torsos.

'J-Jye… Wh-what's the idea…c-coming in here?' As a croak it was pitiful.

He didn't answer, but then since she'd barely heard the words over the boisterous drumming of her heart that wasn't surprising, and the sound of it only got louder once he was close enough for the smooth satin of his boxers to slide along the inside of her thigh. Then his furred chest grazed her nipples, and the decibel level of her chest rose so high every nerve-ending in her body started to vibrate.

'Wh-what're you do-doing?' she gasped as an erotic shudder racked her body.

Under the circumstances she conceded he had every right to grin at such a brain-dead question. 'Take a wild guess, Steff.'

The images in her head were already *way past wild*! But since voicing them was bound to make her look like a tramp, *or worse* a love-sick fool, she fought to make light of the situation.

'Um… Ah…trying to get out of…of sleeping on the sofa?'

Jye's smile was as gentle as the knuckles that brushed her cheek. 'Steff, that's a conservative guess, not the wild one I asked for.'

*Wild,* Stephanie thought frantically. He expected her to be *wild.* Given Jye's vast practical experience with women, and her own very limited one with men, Stephanie wasn't sure she had the know-how to manage *adequate,* much less wild. Oh, sure, her pulse-rate was rampant and her hormones had gone completely feral, but would enthusiasm compensate for inexperience? Making love with Jye would be like going from the learner slopes to the giant slalom.

*But, oh, boy, was she eager to ski!*

'Tell you what,' he said, the hand at the side of her head moving to cup the base of her skull. 'Hold this and I'll give you a clue.'

Glancing down at what he'd shoved in her hand,

Stephanie discovered 'this' to be a box of condoms. A *sealed* box! The significance of which brought her as close to hyperventilating as she'd ever been. It might not represent lifelong commitment, but surely a *whole* box had to mean Jye was thinking beyond just tonight. Her breath wedged in her chest.

'Steff,' he said gently, tilting her chin up. His eyes didn't leave hers as his fingers slowly caressed their way around her neck and his head lowered to hers. 'Concentrate,' he urged. 'This is a clue...'

# CHAPTER NINE

SHE was expecting the kiss to be a passionate and full-bodied assault designed to knock her into the middle of the next century. Instead Jye's mouth was tentative to the point where had she not known better she'd have said it was hesitant. His tongue was so gentle it seemed to tremble across her bottom lip, but perhaps it was only the quaking unsteadiness of her own body creating that impression.

His hands remained planted against the wall, his body arched away from hers, denying the more intimate contact she craved as his mouth repeated its soft almost imaginary kiss over and over. The unhurried, non-intrusive exploration of the outline of her mouth was the most insanely arousing, fascinating thing Stephanie had ever experienced, but she was greedy for even more. Her mind was darting ahead of real time to where his mouth would finally close over hers.

Impatience and desire gnawed at her insides as outwardly her flesh tingled and her nipples hardened to pebbles with risqué anticipation. *Get on with this!* she silently screamed. Yet Jye continued to barely skim and tease her lips, as if she was as fragile as spun crystal and would shatter were he to take complete possession of her mouth and ravish her body.

Okay, so he was right on one count! She *would* shatter under his full-scale sensual assault! But her knees were already trembling, and if he didn't grab hold of her real soon she was going to slump into a frustrated puddle at his feet.

Then, unbelievably, he stopped.

Her eyes were still closed, but she didn't need to open them to know Jye was levering himself away from her; the sensation of cool air over skin which seconds ago had been pressed against hot male flesh was clue enough.

115

Automatically her mind went into rewind, trying to discover what she'd done wrong, and her heart began beating out the rhythm of 'Big Yellow Taxi', chiding her for not appreciating what she'd had when she had it!

'Steff…'

Her name came out as if it was being dragged over sandpaper. And slowly she opened her eyes to find a luminous black pair, set in a handsome, but slightly frowning face.

'Right now I want you something fierce…'

The conviction in his voice froze the air in her lungs, and presumably her vocal cords, since her body's wanton screams of, *Take me! Take me!* never actually made it past her mouth. All those alien emotions were back again, churning through her in a blanket of heat which, combined with desire blazing in his dark eyes, made her feel as if she was being engulfed by a thick, steamy summer's night.

'But…I don't want to hurt you. I'd never forgive myself if I did.' His husky declaration was accompanied by the hypnotic smoothness of his thumb tracing her lower lip with gossamer lightness. 'I need to know you're comfortable with what's happening here, Stephanie. That you can handle it.'

Her sensually blurred brain registered that Jye was trying desperately to be certain she understood the long-term repercussions their sleeping together would have on them. Trying to ensure she wasn't going to get hurt by entertaining ideas that any relationship between them would end in marriage. As touching as that appeared on the surface, Stephanie was enough of a cynic and knew Jye well enough to identify that his *self*-preservation instincts were a large chunk of the motivation behind his nobility.

Oh, Lord, he was such a committed bachelor she didn't know whether she wanted to hit him, laugh or scare him *totally witless* by confessing his warning was futile because she'd already fallen in love with him. No…the last wasn't an option, because the one thing she did know for certain was that she wanted to make love to Jye. Tonight. Now. The slightest hint of the depth of her feeling for him, or mention of the 'L' word, would have him out of the door and out of her life in less than a heartbeat. Suddenly her long-held ultimate desire to marry and have a family had dropped on her priority list to run a pathetically poor second to wanting to experience the pleasure of making love with Jye Fox.

Whatever happened between them tonight would be a once only event, because neither of them would change their views on marriage, yet even knowing that Stephanie couldn't bring herself to walk away from him. Not tonight, anyway... *Not ever*, her heart whispered, knowing it would be Jye who'd ultimately do the walking away.

'Steff...'

She glanced up into his face and immediately saw through the thin veneer of patience he'd held in place for so long. For all his past affairs and his nobility for her feelings, Jye wasn't as nonchalant about what they were proposing to do as he'd have liked her to believe. With that realisation came a faint lifting of her hope levels, and an impish desire to catch him at least as mentally off guard as he'd caught her heart.

'Actually, Jye, I'm *not* comfortable with what's been happening here,' she said boldly, straightening her shoulders. Yanking one of his hands from the wall, she slapped the box of condoms back into it. '*You* can hang onto these! Because you obviously *haven't a clue* what to do with your hands; *I*, however, have big plans for mine!' With that she clamped both of them in his hair and wantonly dragged his startled mouth back to hers!

*Ah!* There was nothing tentative in Jye's kiss now! His mouth merged against hers with a hot, greedy hunger that threatened to consume her as he quickly assumed control of the kiss. His body pressed her back against the wall as his hands quickly scorched over every millimetre of her exposed skin, searing her nerve-endings, vaporising her blood and igniting a passion Stephanie didn't recognise as her own.

Her wanton moan of pleasure as his hand closed under

one breast and a thumbnail grazed its peak had a wicked chuckle grazing her ear. 'Like that, huh?'

'Mmm…' She squirmed as he repeated the action.

'Care to withdraw that accusation that I was clueless?'

'Uh-uh.' She shook her head, rising on her toes to try and reclaim his mouth. 'A person needs motivation to keep bettering themselves.'

Laughing, he evaded her intended kiss and swung her into his arms. 'Oh, don't worry, honey…I'm plenty motivated. You ain't seen nothing yet.'

The cocky arrogance of his statement was as endearing as it was sexually stimulating. Well, *no*, that wasn't entirely true, she mentally amended as the water-filled mattress pitched and waved gently beneath her. 'Endearing' paralleled warm, fuzzy feelings, while sexual stimulation was more like a bushfire raging out of control. Which was exactly how Jye was making her feel as his inquisitive fingers learned her shape and his know-it-all mouth delivered the most sensually scintillating lessons to her until now poorly educated body. Everywhere they touched they ignited a tiny cluster fire, the sparks of which then jumped ahead of the main blaze to inflame another part of her body.

He continued to stoke her passion, until the inner heat intensified to a point where Stephanie thought she'd spontaneously combust with pleasure; these new sensations were addictive. Her body wanted more. Much more. And unashamedly she begged for exactly that. Not merely with words, but with actions. Actions such as her hands' unfettered exploration of the tanned muscular body above hers. Actions that turned his gaze heavy-lidded and his murmured words of approval husky, rough-edged and earthy. His responses filled Stephanie with an exhilarating sense of arrogance in her own femininity, her own sexuality, and dared her to be as wantonly self-indulgent as her desires urged her to be…

Jye felt he was alternately being overpowered and submerged by his most basic instincts. He *knew* he had to slow things down. *Told* himself to do it, to pause and clear his head for a moment. But for all his good intentions he couldn't muster the strength to execute them as layer after layer of both his physical and mental control was stripped from him. He was too weak to withdraw from the heat of the woman beneath him, too weak to deny himself the selfish joy of hearing her moan his name and of watching her beautiful body respond so evocatively to his slightest touch. And much, much too selfish to deny himself the sensations created by her own seemingly fascinated exploration of his body.

The touch of her fingernails combing his chest was almost intangible, yet his insides flared as if she was dragging a match against flint. Who could have imagined her soft, elegant hands would feel so firm and assertive as they moved over his flesh, stroking, moulding, squeezing and caressing until he was certain he'd die from the ecstasy of her touch?

He'd thought he knew Steff better than any woman in this world, which was why when he'd finally succumbed to the overwhelming temptation to satisfy his unexpected sexual curiosity about her he'd never truly been confident of success. Though the arrogantly optimistic part of him had insisted he *couldn't* be imagining the sexual chemistry which had erupted between them during their time on the island, the pessimist in him had been expecting her outright rejection. But even in opting to act on optimism he'd reasoned that he'd need to tread warily, have to gently coax and cajole, be patient with this woman who conservatively believed sex and love were intertwined and naively saw them as a direct route to marriage...

*But, sweet heaven, Stephanie was proving him wrong on all counts!*

There was nothing conservative or naive in the way she either acted or reacted to him. That she was so at ease with her sensuality and sexuality was an act of eroticism in itself; the movements of her body against his were so fluidly smooth he felt as if he was being anointed with warm, scented oil.

There was nothing inhibited about the approving little moans of pleasure she gave as his mouth sought to taste her sweetest nectar. Nor a hint of self-consciousness moments later as she writhed beneath him, clutching at the sheets and demanding that she wanted him. *All of him!*

The temptation to give in to her was greater than any Jye had known. *Ah, what she was doing to him!* No woman had ever affected him so potently, bombarded his emotions so quickly and thoroughly. Yet his ego insisted that he stay in control, not be swept away in the torrent of her sensuality.

In a bid to reassert himself and placate his impatience, he spent several minutes stroking and teasing her passion to the brink of satisfaction, until she was physically trembling and verbally pleading for completion. But passion was a double-edged sword, and there came a time when the unfulfilled promise of pleasure hovered on the edge of pain. A moment when silencing her pleas for complete release with mere kisses was beyond him. Defeated by the craving of his own body, he plunged into her sleek, wet warmth...

In that immeasurable minuscule instant of time Jye was aware of only two things. One was that her throaty growl of satisfaction as she clamped her hands to his buttocks seemed to echo through his head as *Gotcha!* And the second was that his intention to experience her *just once* was shot to ribbons.

Jye scrambled to appear as if his mind hadn't been anywhere but deep in a review of what Sir Frank had just proposed.

'I'd like to be able to think about what you've said, Sir Frank,' he said, seriously doubting he'd retained anything of their two-hour-plus meeting beyond their mutual greetings of 'Good morning'. Even when he'd been staring at spreadsheets of the resort's profits of the last five years all he'd been seeing was the image of Stephanie as he'd left her two hours ago, her nudity semi-covered by a sheet as she lay sprawled and sleeping in his bed. *Her* bed!

'I'd expect nothing less,' the older man said approvingly, before his eyes and smile drifted to the doorway, where Tory had suddenly appeared.

*Or has she been there a while and I simply didn't notice?* Jye wondered, automatically issuing her a polite smile.

As always, the brunette was dressed in designer labels, and breezed into the room with a stride that highlighted the length and tone of her legs. Murmuring an endearment, she dropped a light kiss on her husband's forehead, and for the first time it occurred to Jye that Tory's sexuality was as synthetic as her loving wife routine. He wasn't so much surprised by the fact as by his observation of it. In the past he'd taken pains never to look beyond the packaging where women were concerned. Once a guy started looking below the surface he ran the risk of finding appealing traits and becoming emotionally involved, then the next thing he knew he was doing the bridal waltz and attending childbirth classes.

'Damn!'

He hadn't realised he'd spoken aloud until both Mulligans sent him questioning glances. 'Sorry. Just thought of something I shouldn't have done.'

Sir Frank smirked. *'Not snapped up my proposal straight away?'*

Jye produced the expected smile before saying, 'I never leap without looking, Sir Frank.' *Well, not until last night,* his conscience qualified. 'I'll take on board what you've said this morning and get back to you.'

'By all means. Of you, Jye, I don't expect anything less…' The man's pause was just long enough to qualify as calculated. 'And, to be totally honest, I'd prefer to see Illusions go to the Porter Corporation than one of the less discerning chains.'

Jye didn't rise to the bait and ask what other parties were vying for the resort, though conceivably there could have been half a dozen; Mulligan's tone was enough to convey that Cole Kingston was their main rival.

'As I said earlier,' the older man continued, 'ideally I'd like to see Illusions pass to someone who truly cares about the tourist industry in this country. Though we've been keen competitors in the past, I've enormous respect for Duncan Porter as a businessman. 'He gave what passed as a genuinely rueful smile. 'Unfortunately, though, Jye, we both know that being a businessman myself I can't allow sentiment to cloud my decision on this sale, so if you want to clarify any points, I'll be in my office all afternoon—'

'Oh, darling!' Tory wailed. '*All afternoon.* I wanted to go out on the cruiser for a few hours. I was even going to suggest we take Jye and…um…um…'

'Stephanie,' Jye supplied, fighting a grin.

Tory gave a wave that was halfway between acknowledgment and dismissal. 'Oh, Frank, darling, can't you put off your plans for this afternoon?'

'I'm sorry, Victoria, unfortunately I can't. Still, there's no reason the three of you can't go. Who knows?' He grinned. 'Perhaps a few hours soaking up Illusion's offshore beauty will help Jye reach his decision.'

Jye barely managed to stifle his groan. The last thing he needed was an afternoon being victimised by Tory's vamp. Unfortunately his attempt to gracefully decline the invitation wasn't accepted with anything like grace by Lady Mulligan, and when he held firm with his refusal she resorted to pouts and pleas. It was a ploy which quickly put Jye on the receiving end of an angry glare from Sir Frank, who clearly didn't take kindly to having his spoilt, pampered wife upset.

Jye mentally cursed them both to hell. For all Mulligan's claims that he was first and foremost a businessman, his eccentricities when it came to his wives were well documented; whether an outright refusal to go boating could jeopardise the outcome of their negotiations or not, it wasn't a gamble Jye could afford to take.

'Oh, wonderful!' Tory beamed when he finally accepted.

'Give me a few minutes to change and then we'll head down to the marina.'

'I'm afraid we'll have to make it a bit later. I'm pretty sure Steff will have lunch waiting when I get back. Let's meet there at say…one-thirty?'

Tory looked as crestfallen as it was possible for someone with her well-endowed dimensions to look. 'Oh. Right. I'd forgotten about her.'

It was a pathetic lie, but Jye wished he could make the same claim with even half the conviction. The reality was he had no idea whether Steff would have lunch waiting for him or not, but if she did, chances were he'd be wearing it, not eating it, once she heard what he had to say.

Nevertheless, it had to be said…

'Stephanie, a physical relationship between us just won't work…'

From the minute Jye had walked in the door, looking tense but resolute, with a greeting of, 'Steff, we need to talk…' he'd been mirroring the scene Stephanie had been mentally rehearsing all morning. And, as she'd predicted, he'd given her no opportunity to contradict him by immediately launching into a lengthy and articulate monologue of all the reasons why they'd 'had sex'.

So far he'd blamed isolation, proximity, stress, curiosity and even an *'over-identification with their role as a married couple'* as contributing factors. But, since she'd expected him to cite everything up to and including the unrest in the Middle East for what had occurred, she'd magnanimously remained silent, allowing him to grasp at whatever straws he needed to at this time.

'Well?' he said finally, his expression expectant. 'You must have something to say…'

'Yeah, I do.' Smiling, she walked up to him and seductively slid her palms up his chest. 'Kiss me—'

He backed away so fast she nearly ended up flat on her face; his face was an unsmiling block of dread.

'Haven't you heard a word I've said?' His tone caused

a chill of despair to grab her even before he'd finished speaking. 'What happened last night stays there!'

Oh, God... Jye hadn't been trying to find reasons to justify what had happened because he refused to believe in the concept of love. *He was telling her that last night had been a first and last!* She'd known the minute she'd woken up in bed alone that the next time she saw him he'd be running scared, but, *damn him to hell*, not for a minute had she imagined he'd choose total denial as a way of dealing with things. Here she'd spent all morning trying to decide how long their relationship needed to run before she could tell him how she felt about him without panicking him... And here *he* was disqualifying them both from all future competition!

'Steff?'

'I heard what you said, Jye. But not, apparently, in the context it was intended.' Her voice wasn't as firm as she wanted it to be, but neither was anything else. Her legs had turned to jelly, and her stomach was nauseatingly squishy. Dear God, this couldn't be happening. It...it wasn't fair.

'Steff...I'm sorry. But the wisest thing we can do is admit we acted on impulse and made a mistake last night. Attempting to build on what we shared would only ruin it.'

His *oh, so reasonable*, soft, gentle tone was simultaneously breaking her heart and inciting rage; if she'd had a carving knife she'd have had to toss a coin to decide whether to use it on herself or him first.

'We both know what I'm saying is right, Steff.'

'*Do we?*'

He ignored the challenge of her question. While she'd always been prone to crying over broken romances, she'd previously managed not to do it in front of the jerk who'd done the breaking. And she wouldn't this time either! She might feel ten times worse than she ever had before, but she'd be damned if she'd let the biggest jerk of all know the extent of her devastation. She dug her fingernails into her palms in a bid to remain calm.

'The bottom line is,' Jye was saying, 'that regardless of

how great the sex is—er...*was* between us, we don't want the same things in a relationship. You dream of commitment and I dread it. Neither of us will ever change, no matter how much we might want to pretend otherwise. Trying to take this thing any further would only be compounding what was—'

'*An impulsive mistake!*' she snapped. 'Yeah, all right, Jye, I've got the picture! But just to cut it down to wallet-size,' she said facetiously. 'Answer me this: did this *singular* impulsive mistake occur the first, second, third or *fourth* time we made love?'

'Steff, honey—'

'*Don't touch me,*' she breathed, jerking from his consoling hand. 'Just answer the question! *When do you perceive this impulsive mistake happened?*'

His chest rose and fell with a burdened sigh. 'It happened,' he said, 'when I blurred the long-term value of friendship with the short-term satisfaction of sex; the minute I picked up that box of condoms and walked into your room.'

'Then *you're* the only one who made an impulsive mistake, Jye! Because *I*—' she stabbed a finger against her chest '—slept with you knowing *exactly* what I was doing! I wasn't stupid enough to visualise things leading to a marriage proposal, but I figured our friendship could survive an affair. I tho—'

'An *affair!*' His expression was shocked disbelief. 'We can't have an affair! You don't do affairs!' he informed her. 'Marriage has always been the be all and end all for you. You've always *vowed* you'd never lower yourself to be a man's casual lover.'

'That's right! And the good news is *I haven't broken that vow*! But thanks to *you* my high moral stance against one-night stands has lost all credibility!'

There wasn't enough satisfaction in seeing Jye's handsome face pale at the accusation to defeat the threat of tears; only pride kept them knotted in her throat.

'I...I don't know what to say—'

'No? Well, don't fret over it, because frankly I wouldn't be interested in listening even if you did!' Pivoting on her heel, she hurried to the bedroom.

'Steff, wait!'

She didn't. Nor did she look back at him, tell him to go to hell or even slam the door, and yet Jye felt he'd never been so effectively shut out. Or should that be he'd never so effectively *shut himself out*?

He shifted his gaze back to the small dining table resplendent with white linen cloth, a fruit platter, crystal glasses and an ice bucket of champagne. *Yep, no doubt about it; it was a three-way tie as to whether he was the world's greatest fool, the world's greatest bastard, or the world's greatest martyr...*

# CHAPTER TEN

'HOY, wait for me!'

The sight of Stephanie racing down the pier towards the cruiser brought a wave of relief surging through Jye. And not merely because her presence meant he wasn't going to have to endure an afternoon fighting off Tory Mulligan's advances.

When it had been time for him to leave the cabin and head for the marina, Steff had still been holed up in her room, so Jye had merely knocked on the door and told her what had been arranged for the afternoon. He'd interpreted her lack of response, beyond a vehement, '*Good!* I hope the boat capsizes and you're both taken by sharks,' as a silent refusal to accompany him. For the first time in his professional career he'd been on the verge of putting his personal feelings ahead of business and cancelling the boating excursion in favour of trying to execute damage control on the friendship he valued above all others; all that had stopped him was the knowledge there'd be no reasoning with Stephanie until she'd calmed down... He'd figured he had about two decades to wait.

A sideways glance at Tory as Steff bounded onto the deck revealed that, unlike him, she was far from pleased by the unexpected last-minute arrival of his 'wife'. Nor did she make any pretence of the fact, scowling in response to Stephanie's cheerful greeting.

'What are *you* doing here?' she demanded.

'*Excuse me?*' Stephanie was dressed in shorts and peering from beneath a faded baseball cap; even so, her expression and tone would have put royalty in their place. It clearly surprised Tory, but not to the point of an apology.

'Jye said you weren't coming,' she said, in a tone suggesting she'd liked that arrangement. Shooting Jye an accusing look, she added, 'He said you were sick. *Again.*'

Without missing a beat, Stephanie backed his lie. 'I was.'

'Then why are you here?' Tory challenged. 'I hardly think you should be out tearing about in the hot sun and contemplating a cruise. It's obvious you suffer from a less than robust constitution, what with you being so pathetically skinny and all.'

The barb had made a direct hit, and, forewarned of Steff's potentially scorching comeback by the glint that lit her eyes, Jye jumped to intervene. 'Oh, Steff's usually healthy as a horse!' he said heartily. 'But you know how morning sickness can be. She—' He broke off the instant he realised Tory was no longer the object of Steff's outraged glare.

'She's *pregnant?*' Tory's surprise was as sharp as the visual daggers Steff was hurling at him.

Taking a wild guess that he'd made a tactical error here, he hastily tried to save the situation. 'Well, eh…that is, we *think* she is. Er…she could be. Well, might be. Er… It hasn't been confirmed yet. Has it, honey?'

'No, *sweetheart*, which is why I wanted to keep it a secret.' As smiles went, the one directed at Jye came under the heading of 'murderous'.

'*Oops.*' He tried for a sheepish grin. 'Still, there's no reason to get upset, I'm sure Tory won't spread it around. Will you, Tory?'

'*I doubt I'd ever be that desperate for conversation!*' The scathing tone was accompanied by a shudder and a frigid stare. 'If you'll excuse me, Jye, I'll let you two sort out your domestics differences in private. And I really think it would be best if you could convince your wife not to accompany us. I don't want my afternoon ruined because the expectant mother is throwing up over the side.'

'Oh, don't worry, Lady Mulligan,' Stephanie said. 'I think the fact I haven't thrown up since stepping aboard *proves* I've got an exceptionally strong stomach!'

Forcing a laugh in the faint hope Tory would mistake

the remark as a joke, Jye grasped Steff's elbow and hurriedly steered her towards the stern. 'Don't let her get to you,' he muttered. 'She's not worth it.'

'*She's* not the one getting to me! Why the hell did you say I was pregnant?'

He should have known she wouldn't let that one go through to the wicketkeeper. 'It was the first thing that came into my head to account for why you keep getting sick.'

'*So quit saying I'm sick!*'

'Look, I had to have some explanation for why you weren't here. Telling her we'd had a tiff would've been on a par to presenting her with a million dollars. To be honest, I wasn't expecting you to show up.'

'*To be honest,*' she parroted. 'I wasn't intending to; I'm not exactly in the mood to churn out favours.'

'But you're here anyway. ' He smiled then, unable to resist reaching out and grazing his knuckles along the creamy smoothness of her cheek. 'Thanks, Steff. I appreciate it.'

'Well, don't!' She jerked away, folding her arms. 'I'm only here because this deal is important to Porter's and especially to Duncan. Godfather wouldn't appreciate it if we blew it because we let personal differences get the better of us. Besides,' she added, looking reluctant, 'I owe you an apology.'

'*You do?*'

'Don't get too excited,' she warned wryly, 'I'm giving it grudgingly. But the thing is, it wasn't fair of me to put all the blame for what happened on you. It's not like you didn't give me a chance to back out last night. And if I'd been listening to my brains instead of my hormones I *would've*,' she asserted, her gaze narrowing. 'I guess I overreacted because in the past I've only ever slept with two guys—'

'Steff, stop! I don't need to hear this.' Hell, he didn't even want to *think* about Stephanie in another guy's arms!

'No. Of course.' She bit her lip, undoubtedly feeling

embarrassed, and shrugged. 'Anyway, I just wanted you to know that…well, you've done me a big favour.'

'I have?'

She nodded. 'I've been so obsessed with commitment and permanency in my past relationships that I've probably deprived myself of some really great sex, and—'

'*Stephanie!*'

'What?' Her eyes were wide and puzzled.

'Whaddya mean *what*?' He glared at her. 'Do you realise what you're saying?'

'I'm saying that you've been right all along, Jye,' she responded calmly. 'Variety *is* the spice of life. And…' the wink and smirk she gave him should have been 'X'-rated '…thanks to you, from now on Stephanie Elizabeth Bernadette Worthington is shopping for heartburn!'

Having given up on the pipedream of getting any sleep on the sofa, Jye stared at the ceiling.

It was all talk, of course. When push came to shove, there was no way Stephanie was going to crawl into bed with a guy solely in the name of sex. She wasn't the type. And he ought to know. He'd known Steff since she was six years old and been intimately acquainted with the kind of woman who did exactly that since he'd been sixteen. Her announcement today had simply been a self-defence mechanism to convince both of them that last night was no big deal, he assured himself.

Still, it was a damn good thing they were stuck on this island and for all intents and purposes married, because history showed Stephanie was notorious for being impulsive. If they'd been on the mainland it wasn't inconceivable that she might have rushed out and attempted to *spice up her life* before she'd fully considered the consequences. Hopefully, by the time they sealed the deal with Mulligan, she'd be back to promoting eternal love and the picket fence ideal.

'Jye…are you awake?'

He sat bolt upright at the sound of her softly spoken question.

As she moved nearer, the flow of moonlight through the partially opened patio blinds lent a silver glow to the expanse of shapely bare legs beneath an over sized T-shirt and the beautiful face beneath a tousled cap of blonde hair. Jye clenched his teeth against a spike of arousal.

'Can we talk for a minute?'

Although Jye's libido was suggesting something it would much rather they do, and for a lot longer than a minute, he nodded. He'd had more than his share of women approach his bed in the middle of the night, their attire ranging from erotically designed negligées to well filled out birthday suits, but he couldn't recall one of them looking as sexy or as tempting as Stephanie did now.

Biting down on a groan, produced from rising hopes he knew he shouldn't be entertaining, he quickly pulled his leg away when her neat little backside brushed against it as she sat down.

'I'm not quite sure how to say this…'

The hesitancy in her voice set his pulse throbbing.

'Say what, Steff?' he asked hoarsely.

'It's about last night…and what you said on the boat?'

'What about last night?' More than his pulse was throbbing now.

She shot him a quick, shy look, before dipping her head. 'Well, I'm worried that maybe you've jinxed me. Well, *us*, actually.'

'Jinxed us? How?'

'By telling Tory I was pregnant.'

It took Jye a full second to register what she was saying. When he did, his heart froze somewhere in the region of his throat, handicapping his vocal cords.

'Y-you're saying…y-you might *really* be pr—be preg—' He gulped his heart back into his chest. *'Pregnant?'*

'Oh, darn it! I *knew* I shouldn't have mentioned it. Now you're worried too.'

*Worried?* Who was she kidding? *Catatonic with shock was more like it.*

'Please, Jye,' she urged. 'Don't panic. There's only a *very* remote chance that I am.'

'But…but we used condoms. Why would you think—? Oh, hell! One came off after we…'

Her silver-capped head nodded. 'I know we thought it was funny at the time. But I was thinking about last night, and on reflection…well…'

Her choice of words momentarily shut down Jye's mind to the fear of possible fatherhood. *She'd* been thinking about last night too. No, she'd been *reflecting* on last night. The word didn't suggest she was ruing the incident, but viewing it almost wistfully. Like he'd been doing. Constantly. *All day.*

'Look, Jye,' she continued, dragging his mind from its steamy images. 'I'm probably overreacting. In fact I'm sure I wouldn't have even *thought* about the possibility of being pregnant if you hadn't said what you had to Tory today.'

She patted his leg with what Jye considered an overkill of reassurance, but the heat of her hand on his bare thigh was enough for his increased heart-rate to be attributed to things other than impending fatherhood. Yet when his own hand settled on hers she shot to her feet and gave an obviously forced laugh.

'Honestly, I'm being silly! The chances of me being—' She broke off with a shake of her head. 'Oh, look, it's all too ridiculous! Forget I mentioned it and—'

'*Forget you mentioned it!* Hell, Stephanie, you might as well ask me to stop breathing!' He leapt from the sofa and started pacing the floor.

*Stephanie was possibly pregnant with his child.* He tried to picture her trim flat belly swollen with his child. He couldn't. Yet at the same time he felt a flash of high-octane excitement enter his blood. He thought… He thought… *Well, dammit, he couldn't think!* Not with the racket of his pounding heart. Just breathing was hard enough. He continued to pace the darkened room, trying desperately to get his head around the situation.

At the evidence of Jye's obvious and extreme agitation Stephanie was consumed by guilt. What she'd told him wasn't beyond the realms of possibility, but she'd been acting purely out of bitchiness in saying she was worried. She wasn't. The probability of them having created a child was almost as remote as Jye deciding he'd fallen madly in love with her. But because he'd hurt her so much she'd wanted to punish him.

He'd teased her with glimpses of how well he'd fulfil the role of husband, made love to her as if she was the most precious person to him in the whole world, and then turned around and publicly announced that they were having a child. It was as if he'd practically handed her her wildest dream then cruelly snatched it away. She hated him for it, yet at the same time loved him too much to enjoy his suffering. There was no satisfaction in watching his tortured reaction.

'Jye...please. There's no point getting stressed out. I...I'm sure I'm not pregnant.'

'No, you're not. Sure, that is.' His mouth was a grim line as he stared at her.

'Okay. But...but it's highly unlikely.'

'"Unlikely" isn't impossible.'

He stopped pacing to come and stand in front of her. It took all her will-power not to take hold of his very serious face in her hands and kiss the concern from it.

'When will you know for sure?' he asked tightly.

'Um...er...' She pulled up a quick mental calendar. 'Nine or ten days.'

His eyes darkened as he studied her. 'Okay, then. Well, if you are...pregnant, I'm...' His Adam's apple bounced from the effects of a huge gulp. 'I'm...willing to marry you.'

Her heart got more stupidly excited than her brain at the *oh, so noble* offer. 'If you ask me, I'll say no.'

'What? Why?'

It both amused and irritated her that he could look so stunned. '*Because,*' she said dryly, 'I'm not into human sacrifice, Jye.'

If possible he looked even more affronted. 'Are you saying being married to me would be a sacrifice?'

'Oh, for God's sake, Jye! You've made it abundantly clear that you have never wanted to get married—'

'Yeah, but I meant voluntarily. This is different. If you're carrying my child then marrying you is obligatory. In fact I'd be prepared to marry anyone in these circumstan—*grr-rugh!*'

As Jye's backside bounced off the floor, Stephanie followed up her unexpected right hook with an angry, colourful description of his heritage, punctuating it with a series of wild barefooted kicks to random areas of his stunned form.

'As far as I'm concerned...' *kick* '...you can shove your obligations...' *kick* '...in your rear, Jye Fox!' *Kick.* 'I wouldn't marry you if I was ten months pregnant with quintuplets and already had *seven* of your kids! An—'

Jye grabbed her ankle mid-strike, unbalancing her enough so that she tumbled down onto him. Immediately she started fighting to get free.

'Let go, you son of—'

'Shh, Steff. Settle down, honey.'

'Don't *honey* me, you...' she slammed a fist into his shoulder '...you insensitive, arrogant, over-sexed piece of slime!' His shoulder copped another jab. '*Let me go!*'

'No! Ouch! Steff, stop it! *Now!*' he insisted, grabbing her wrists.

'Why should I?'' she demanded, trying to wriggle free.

'Because it's not good for the baby for you to get over-excited.'

Instantly she stilled. Her eyes locked to his, her confusion and distress the only two emotions he could clearly identify in her face.

'Jye... I—'

'What?'

She shook her head. 'Nothing. It's just that, even if I am pregnant, what little understanding I do have on the subject tells me I can handle a little mild exercise.'

'Well, since I know next to nothing on the subject, I'll take your word for it. But...' he rubbed his jaw '...it's *my* health I'm concerned about. And, since I instinctively seem to be reluctant to defend myself against a possibly pregnant woman, do you think you could rein in the homicidal urges until we know for certain?'

She sprang out of his lap to tower above him, her hands on her hips hitching her already short T-shirt even higher. The intimidating step closer she took brought her beautiful bare legs to within centimetres of his touch.

'*Instinctive reluctance*, my foot! Your instincts are so slow you never even *saw* me coming until I laid you out!' A smug grin made her eyes sparkle.

'You're right. I didn't,' Jye conceded, but he wasn't just talking about her powerful right. In the last few days Stephanie had managed to unbalance him both physically and emotionally to such an extent that not even the idea he might be destined for fatherhood was as devastating as he would have expected it to be a little over a week ago; *although it should have been!* Parenthood definitely wasn't a project he'd deemed he was ever going to take on. Steff's announcement should have had him scared witless instead of merely numb with bemusement.

Of course, maybe some measure of his calmness was due to the fact Stephanie hadn't jumped at his pledge to marry her if indeed she was pregnant. But, hell! *Couldn't she have shown a little gratitude for the offer?* Only a matter of days ago she'd been willing to marry that jerk Carey for no better reason than imagining herself in love with him!

A few moments later she muttered a barely audible good-night, but Jye knew even if he'd suddenly been presented with the most comfortable bed on earth, then shot full of ether, there wasn't a hope in Hades he was going to be able to sleep now. Which meant he could either sit around in a dry sweat, brooding over something he couldn't do anything about, or he could try and focus on the reason he'd come to Illusion Island in the first place and take positive steps towards getting Mulligan to move from the ridiculous price he was asking for the complex.

Deciding his second option was infinitely the wisest was one thing; being able to do it was another matter all together.


'Come on, Stephanie, my girl,' she muttered to her reflection. 'Go with guts. You can't stay in the bathroom all morning.'

*Oooh, but if only I could!* she thought, drawing a fortifying breath as she reached for the door handle. *If only—*

She reared backwards as a loud rap from the other side of the timber vibrated along her arm.

'Breakfast's here, Steff!'

'Um…er, good. Thanks. I'll be right out.'

It actually took her another five minutes to screw up the courage to face Jye, a ridiculous situation considering she was supposed to be a mature adult and she'd known him all her life. Equally ridiculous and even more irritating was the way her dumb heart flipped over when he looked up as she slid into the chair opposite his at the small table.

'I hope you got some sleep last night, because I didn't,' he said with a wry smile that didn't work. He looked tired—no, *exhausted*, and much as she would have liked to pretend the discomfort of the sofa was solely responsible for his obviously sleepless night, her conscience wouldn't let her.

Only a real bitch would have done what she had to him last night, and here she'd been casting aspersions on Tory! Filled with remorse, she instinctively reached across and trapped his hand beneath hers. She felt his tremor of surprise even before his dark eyes widened with the same reaction, but almost instantly he leaned back in his chair, effectively drawing out of her reach.

Stifling the overwhelming sense of rejection she knew she had no business feeling, she forced herself to smile, as if his action was of no consequence. The time to start pulling herself together was right how. If she wanted to maintain her friendship with Jye in the wake of this debacle she was going to have to get her act together. And the first thing she had to do was apologise to him.

'I'm sorry, Jye. I shouldn't have dumped all that on you last night. Not when you're in the middle of crucial negotiations. It was thoughtless and unprofessional of me. Duncan would skin me alive if he knew.'

One dark eyebrow arched in scepticism. 'If he knew *what*? That we'd slept together, or that you'd alerted me to the possible repercussions of that action?'

'Don't be dense. The latter, of course. Duncan and I both know your libido has never compromised your performance in the boardroom.'

Pleased with how objective she'd sounded, she gasped as Jye slammed a fist onto the table, up-ending the jug of orange juice.

'Thanks for reminding me of that, Steff! I'll be damned sure to point that out to him if I happen to blow this deal and it turns out you are pregnant!'

'I'm *not* pregnant!'

'You might be!'

'There's only a *minute* chance of that,' she said, telling herself she *wasn't* secretly wishing it was greater. 'There's no need for you to start freaking out about it until we're sure.'

'I'm not "freaking out about it".'

'Well, you could've fooled me! A minute ago when I touched your hand you acted like I had bubonic plague!' Blinking against the tears welling in her eyes, she hurried on, forcing a rational voice. 'Let's wait until we see what happens. Then, if I am pregnant, we can decide whether or not to tell Duncan who the father is.'

Jye reared up from his chair, again rocking the table and this time sending glasses tumbling.

*'There's no deciding about it!'* he roared, certain every blood vessel in his brain had just burst with fury. Never

had he so wanted to kill someone with his bare hands. Damn her, she had every right to be frozen in her chair.

'Understand...this...Stephanie.' He'd lowered his voice, but was advancing on her with every enunciated word. 'If you're having my child, Duncan *and everybody else* is bloody well going to know *I'm* the father.'

Bending with deliberate slowness, he clamped one hand in a puddle of OJ and the other on the back of her chair, effectively trapping her.

'Are you receiving the message on this, Stephanie Elizabeth Bernadette Worthington? Because I have absolutely no intention of standing silently on the sidelines while you go the route of abandoned single mother.'

'B-but...but you know Duncan frowns...on...on us parading our...eh...personal relationships in the office.' She swallowed hard, her elegant neck arching as she tipped her head back to put some distance between them. Jye countered her effort by leaning closer.

'Stuff Duncan and his frown,' he told her, leaning nearer her beautiful but startled face. 'And forget any ideas you have about refusing to marry me, because no child of mine is going to grow up without having two parents.'

'A...a person doesn't have to be married to be a parent, Jye.'

They were practically nose to nose. So close he could have counted every spiky lash that surrounded her astounded eyes. So close that suddenly strangling her wasn't the foremost thought in his fatigued scrambled brain. As the smell of her shampoo mingled with the scent he recognised as uniquely her, he could no more have stopped his hungry mouth's journey to her lips than he could have walked his way back to the mainland.

When his tongue encountered the soft moisture of her lower lip the desire which tore through him was visceral. He groaned, closing his eyes with the glorious intensity of it.

'Oomph!'

For the second time in less than twelve hours she caught

him off guard. On this occasion with a double-palmed shove to the chest which caused him to stagger backwards, but at least allowed him to remain on two feet.

Immediately she sprang to hers. 'Back off, Jye,' she warned him. 'Okay, fine! If I'm pregnant I'll make sure you get all the credit,' she said snidely. 'But *don't* think you can dupe me into marrying you and turning you into the last living martyr with a session of hot, sexy kisses,' she railed. 'Because I *never* repeat my mistakes.'

Stephanie's reaction struck him as a case of protesting too much, and he made no effort to hide his amusement.

'Liar,' he teased. 'You forget; I've eaten your cooking more than once.'

'Very funny! But I'll give you a tip, Jye... I wouldn't go eating it again if I were you, because the next time you say I've made something too bitter it won't be because I've forgotten to use sugar!

'Now, will you just do us both a favour and cut all this...this *crap* about you wanting to marry me so we can concentrate on closing this damn deal? The sooner I'm back in the sanctuary of my own house, the better!'

'I'm as anxious as you are to get home, Stephanie. But, for the record, I never said I *wanted* to marry you,' he felt it necessary to point out in response to her stubbornness on the issue. 'I said I *would* marry you. There's a difference, you know!'

Stephanie was almost apoplectic as she struggled to rein in a sudden lust for blood that would have turned a vampire's stomach. *How could a man of Jye's intellect be so...so emotionally retarded?* Oooh! She was so mad, if she let her knee have its way he'd spend the rest of his life with chipmunk cheeks!

Oblivious to her vicious thoughts, he brought the vital parts of his anatomy into potential peril when he shoved a slim blue file under her nose.

'Here,' he said gruffly. 'This is my latest offer for Illusions. Take a look at it while I have a shower. We're due to meet Mulligan in just over an hour.'

The comment distracted her from her anger as nothing else would have.

'You want *me* to come to the meeting? Why? I'm only here for window-dressing. I've never been involved in a purchase before.'

He shrugged. 'Mulligan doesn't know that. I'm hoping that it might look like we're a little more committed to the deal by increasing our numbers.'

'But I wouldn't be able to contribute anything. If anything, I'm likely to open my mouth and screw the whole thing.'

'That's garbage, Steff. You've been listening to Duncan discuss the whys and wheres of purchasing hotels since you were six years old.' His coal-black eyes fixed on hers. 'I want you there, Stephanie.'

The conviction behind his words made her wish he'd left out the qualifying word 'there'. If he had, she was honest enough to admit she'd have probably stripped naked on the spot and thrown herself at him. She pushed the too tempting image aside, for fear she'd act on it.

'Fair enough. You want me in full power-suit mode?'

Considering the way Jye was feeling, it was a loaded question, but he bit back the all too earthy response that automatically rolled to the tip of his tongue and nodded. 'We might as well go in all guns blazing from this point; the bad news is Kingston's lurking in the background, undoubtedly ready to part with a ridiculously obscene sum.'

'Mulligan could be lying about Kingston in the hope you'll jump at his offer. He knows how Duncan feels about foreign ownership,' she said sagely.

'True. I believe him when he says he'd genuinely like Porter's to get Illusions, but I'm uneasy about trying to put a guesstimate on the price of his sentiment. I figure he'll give us maybe two chances to negotiate a figure he likes, and if we're not in the ball park he'll take whatever Kingston's offering.'

Stephanie frowned. 'Duncan was adamant that he didn't want Kingston beating him on this.'

'I know.' He dragged a hand wearily across the back of his neck. 'But I'm not Duncan; I can't come at buying at a price that means it'll take us twenty-five years to turn a decent profit. So where does that leave you?'

She could count on one hand the number of times she'd seen Jye less than confident about a deal—which, she figured, put her in an élite group of around one. Confidence was definitely a big part of Jye's public persona, and it came as an enormous relief that even though their friendship was currently on such shaky ground he hadn't entirely closed his real feelings off to her.

'I guess,' she said, 'it leaves me relying on your gut instincts.' She smiled. 'If it's any consolation, the day I left Duncan said he had absolute confidence in your judgement.'

He raised a sceptical eyebrow. 'In light of recent events I wouldn't have expected *you* to advocate I follow my instincts.'

'I was referring to your *business* instincts, Jye. Now, unless you want to get into another argument I suggest you go take your shower.'

Jye was magnificent!

All through the long, intense meeting with Sir Frank, his demeanour remained so sedate that an unsuspecting onlooker would have assumed him to be disinterested; yet with nothing more than a raised eyebrow or a subtly pointed question he would have the older man retracting or amending an earlier fact or figure which edged the negotiations in favour of the Porter Corporation. On several occasions he evoked Steff's opinion on various issues, but in such a way that she couldn't help but be confident in her response. His support of her comments and his unfailing ability to produce figures to back up her claims when Sir Frank questioned them filled her with a new admiration for just how intimately knowledgeable he was of all facets of the Porter Corporation's operations. There was little doubt Godfather's faith in him was well placed, but when Sir

Frank finally leaned back in his seat after five hours of coffee-fuelled discussion and said he was satisfied with Porter's offer the pride Steff felt for Jye was deeply personal rather than professional.

Her first instinct was to leap from her chair and throw her arms around his neck, but, taking her lead from Jye, who'd not so much as looked in her direction, she limited her enthusiasm to a smile as businesslike as the one he directed to Sir Frank.

'Well, then,' the older man said, 'I think this calls for a celebration. Shall we say dinner at eight?'

'Sorry, Sir Frank,' Jye said. 'But we need to head back to the mainland as soon as possible. Any chance you could arrange to have your chopper pilot fly us to Cairns airport this afternoon?'

Jye's request brought excruciating pain to every part of Stephanie's body. It was over. Done. Mission accomplished. In a few short hours her pseudo-marriage to Jye Fox would be finished. No more fights. No more kisses. No more loving.

*Good!*

The sooner she got her life back to normal the better. Jye wanted to end the fiasco as quickly as possible; immediately, if not sooner. So did she. She was glad it was over. *She was.* She'd played her part and her godfather would be ecstatic that the deal was all but delivered, if not signed and sealed, but that was up to both companies' legal teams; her part in all this was done.

Gosh. It was such a relief to have the ordeal over, she couldn't even think of what she needed to do next... Pack. Yes, packing was the first priority. Oh, and she'd have to call Ellee or Duncan to meet her plane at Sydney airport. No, no...not her godfather—he'd want to talk business, probably want the three of them to have dinner together. She didn't want to have to face Jye over another meal.

'Stephanie...a toast.'

She blinked at the sound of Sir Frank's voice and discovered a champagne glass full of orange juice being held towards her. Her confusion must have showed because the man said, 'You won't want to drink alcohol if you're pregnant, my dear.'

*I'm not pregnant!* she screamed silently, but, acting on autopilot, smilingly accepted the glass and raised it in the man's toast of their successfully negotiated deal. She'd taken only two sips when Tory *slunk* her way into the room in an untied beach robe and bikini that left one wondering why she'd even bothered to put it on. Before the brunette had even pouted at having been omitted from the opening of the champagne, Stephanie set her glass aside and excused herself, saying she had to start packing.

Jye was murmuring agreement, and eagerly began packing documents into his briefcase, but the thought of being alone in the cabin with him was more than she felt able to cope with right now.

'No, eh...*darling.*' She forced a smile. 'One of us should stay on and properly celebrate the deal. It's okay... I can pack for both of us.'

Ignoring Jye's look of promised retribution, she shook hands with Sir Frank, bidding him a suitably polite and cheerful goodbye, then steeled herself to meet Tory's feline gaze.

'Goodbye, Lady Mulligan.' She smiled, then flicked her eyes briefly over the copious amount of exposed plastic-enhanced flesh. 'It's certainly been a real...*revelation* meeting you.' With that she pivoted on her heel and headed for the door.

Jye was there to open it for her, but his slowness in doing so drew her gaze to his face. 'What's the matter?' he asked, in a voice only she would hear, looking genuinely confused.

'Nothing.'

'Why are you angry with me?'

'Why would I be angry with you? You've just pulled off a terrific deal.'

'*We* pulled it off. I couldn't have done it without you.'

Because she suddenly felt like crying, she smiled. 'Whatever. The good news is it's done, and we're only a couple of hours away from ending this charade. And on that cheerful thought, I'm off to pack!'

# CHAPTER ELEVEN

WHEN their flight landed in Sydney, Stephanie practically ran to the luggage carousel, telling Jye that the deep freeze treatment she'd been treating him to since they'd left Cairns airport hadn't lost any of its bite on the trip south.

'What?' she snapped, not looking at him.

'How about we go get something to eat before we go home?'

'Thanks, but I'm not hungry.'

'You must be; you haven't eaten all day.'

This time she did look at him. 'That would be because I wasn't hungry. When I am, I'll eat. Now, just let me find my luggage.'

Sighing, he raked his hair, wondering how to deal with her in a way that wouldn't get him arrested for murder given that they were in a public place.

'Look, Steff, I know what happened the other night has upset you—hell, it's thrown me for a loop too! But we have to decide where we're going to go from here—'

'I'm going home,' she said, her eyes not leaving her bag as the conveyor belt brought it nearer. 'You can please yourself.'

'That's not what I mean and you know it. We can't just pretend the other night never happened,' he said, reaching for her bag at the instant she did and discovering that even when she was driving him nuts touching her could make him forget even his own name. Stephanie pulled away as if she'd encountered slime.

In a bid to keep what little pride she still had Stephanie made a production of checking the outside of the case for damage. She was still so emotionally off balance from the events of the last few days that she doubted she'd be capable of even the most minimal conversation. Although with images of their night of passion continuing to roll unbidden and non-stop through her mind it was far more likely she'd either burst out crying or kick Jye so hard she'd both cripple him and make his nose bleed.

'Steff…'

'What?'

'Look at me.'

With her foot itching and the tightness of her throat growing into an unswallowable lump, she took a moment to psyche herself into calmness, before raising her head. It was a wasted moment; one glance into those coal-black eyes had her heating up in places she only ever wanted Jye to touch. Unable to hold his gaze and her dignity at the same time, she turned her head and fortuitously saw the perfect distraction.

'Jye, look; there's your bag.'

'Forget the bloody bag!' Grabbing her shoulders, he brought her face to face to him. 'We can't avoid discussing what happened at the resort.'

'Well, of course not,' she said, marvelling at how even her voice was. 'Duncan's going to expect a detailed report of the transaction. Tomorrow morning's good for me…'

'Stop being obtuse, damn it!' he snapped. 'I'm talking about us sleeping together!' Frustration elevated his voice, causing several heads to turn in their direction.

'Geez, Jye, why don't you just have them announce it over the airport PA?' she hissed, red-faced and furious.

'I will, if that's what it's going to take to get you to stop ignoring the situation. There's noth— Damn! What's *she* doing here?'

Stephanie followed his glare to the glass entrance doors of the domestic terminal, where the sight of Ellee scanning the crowd immediately sent relief flooding through her.

'Ellee!' she yelled, her intended wave aborted when Jye grabbed her arm.

'I would've dropped you home,' he told her testily.

She pulled her arm free. 'Don't be ridiculous. You live in the entirely opposite direction. The cab fare would've been exorbitant.'

'When did you worry about the cost of cab fares? Since your car was stolen yours have always been the highest in the entire company.'

'A point *you've* always taken issue with,' she countered. 'There's really no pleasing you, is there?'

'Now that's not entirely true, Stephanie. You pleased me just fine the other night...several times.'

His seductive tone caused her pulse to hitch, despite her best efforts to appear indignant. 'I'm not interested in discussing the other night. *Ever.*'

'Well, that's too bad, because in a few months we could very well find ourselves discussing birthing techniques!'

*'I'm not pregnant.'*

'We hope,' he said. 'Unfortunately there's an old adage about hope not proving a reliable form of contraception.'

'Hi, you guys!' For Stephanie, Ellee's bright, friendly arrival couldn't have been more perfectly timed. Not only did it spare her having to respond to Jye, but it coincided with his luggage vanishing into the bowels of the building for the second time and granting her the opportunity for a speedy escape.

'So, Jye,' Ellee said, 'how was the trip?'

'Successful,' Stephanie answered, determined to sever any conversation before it could get started. 'Here.' She shoved her carry-on at Ellee, then seized her elbow. 'Okay, let's go. Where are you parked?'

If Jye offered any response to her mumbled, 'See ya.' Stephanie didn't hear it over the emotional temper tantrum going on inside her, but she felt his eyes on her all the way to the exit of the terminal.

'What's going on?' Ellee asked.

'Nothing.'

'Then what's your rush and why are you squeezing my elbow hard enough to cut off circulation to my lower arm?'

Grimacing, Steff released her hold. 'Sorry.'

'Okay...what gives with you and Jye?'

'Nothing.'

'Knock it off, Stephanie. This is *me* you're talking to. I

know when you're upset. And I didn't imagine the tension ricocheting between you and Jye. Now, accept that not only is confession good for the soul, but it will also stop me nagging you and you'll feel a whole lot better.'

Her friend grinned as she let out a resigned sigh. 'Okay, Ellee, you're right; I am upset... Brad Carey was staying at the Illusion Resort.'

Ellee's jaw almost bounced off the pavement. 'Holy cow! You're kidding me, right?'

'Nope. Brad and his newly acquired wife were there.'

Stephanie told herself she wasn't deliberately deceiving her best friend; it was just that she wasn't up to discussing what had happened between her and Jye with anyone yet. He'd taken her most precious dream and destroyed it by making her realise she only wanted it with him. Dear Lord, even *thinking* about it had her on the brink of tears, and for the time being it was better that Ellee think she was still upset because Brad had married Karrie. Having fallen in love with a man who'd merely married as a career choice was marginally less ego-abusive than having to admit falling for an anti-marriage, commitment-phobic bachelor whose interest in women ran to a long string of curvaceous bimbos with single digit IQs. *Especially when she hadn't been able to hold it beyond one night in the sack!*

'By the way, thanks for picking me up,' she said. 'It's my treat for Chinese on the way home.'

'Nice try, but forget the Chinese, Steff,' Ellee said dryly. 'The only thing I want you to feed me are facts. *All of them.* Now...what's going on with you and Jye?'

'I told you...*nothing.*'

'Exactly. So now try telling me *something.*'

'Ellee, there's nothing to tell. Really. No drama; things just got a bit awkward when Brad turned up at the resort.'

'Why?'

'Why, what? Why was Brad at the resort?'

'Why were things awkward?'

'God, Ellee! *Why do you think?*' Stephanie snapped, deciding offence was her best defence in the face of such tenacious curiosity. 'It wasn't exactly easy being on the same island as him under the circumstances.

'And, if you'll recall, Jye wasn't thrilled when I told him how I felt about Brad; so naturally, with Brad and Karrie on the island, all he did was constantly keep reminding me they were *married* and that I was there to work. So I guess if you sense tension between Jye and me it's because I resent him treating me like I'm some sort of unprofessional bimbo!'

Stephanie mentally congratulated herself on her truthful yet ambiguous response, but when Ellee's expression suggested she wasn't entirely convinced she added a further tidbit.

'And it didn't help any either that Sir Frank's latest wife is one of Jye's exes.'

'Holy cow!'

'Yep! A whole herd of them,' she prattled on theatrically. 'I tell you, Ellee, Jye and I have done nothing but walk on eggshells for days; is it any wonder we're both a bit on edge? It wasn't easy concentrating on business when we were both being confronted by past emotional baggage.'

'Holy cow, Steff, no wonder you've got bags under your eyes. I bet you're glad it's all over, eh?'

'Yeah,' she said. 'I am.'

Well, so much for sticking to the truth…

The last drowsy remnants of what little sleep she'd managed to get during the night vanished at the sight of the man frowning at her from her front doorstep. 'What are you doing here?'

'You always open your door at this hour in PJs without asking who it is?' Jye growled.

'At this hour,' she said, trying to ignore the fact he looked better in the flesh than he had in all her sleepless fantasies, 'it seemed safe to assume the only people likely to be pounding on my door would be firefighters coming to evacuate me because the house was ablaze.'

'I hope that doesn't mean you've already started cooking breakfast,' he said, somehow managing to manoeuvre his way past her to lead the way down her hall. ''Cause I stopped by the bakery and picked up some pastries for us.'

'Why would you do that?'

'It'll save you the time of cooking breakfast. You know what a stickler the old man is for punctuality.'

Feeling as if she'd woken up in a parallel universe, or at the very least a dream, she closed her eyes and shook her head to clear it. But, no, when she looked again the same incredibly sexy man who'd kept her awake all night with either rage or tears was poking through her kitchen pantry.

'What's going on? I thought we were supposed to meet with Duncan at seven-thirty *at the office*.'

'We are. But I decided it made sense for me to pick you up.'

*Sense?* He had to be kidding. He lived way over the other side of the harbour and only twenty minutes from the office; from her place it was a forty-five-minute drive even if there wasn't a pile-up on the Harbour Bridge.

'Jye, are—?'

'Where's your radio, Steff? I might as well listen to the overseas news while I'm getting breakfast.'

Deciding she wasn't up to dealing with this until she'd had a shower to unscramble her brain, she meekly pointed to the sound system in her living room. 'Knock yourself out, but don't bother fixing me anything. I'll just have coffee.'

'You have to eat, Steff.'

'Not if I don't want to.'

As if she hadn't spoken he continued setting two places at the table. 'Where do you keep your decaf?'

'I don't have decaf.'

'Oh…well, in that case I guess it'll have to be tea. You can pick up some decaf today.'

'No, I won't,' she countered, becoming irritated by the way he was commandeering her kitchen and giving orders. 'I happen to hate decaf. In fact I think it should be banned for devaluing the word "coffee". I don't even breathe of a morning until I've got at least one and a half cups of that noble beverage in me.'

He shrugged. 'So, from now on you'll have to practise

breathing from the second you wake up. But don't worry, as far as I know no one's ever died from coffee withdrawal.'

'Really? Well, the number of people who have died at the hands of someone in desperate need of a caffeine fix is in immediate danger of increasing by one.'

He turned a fleeting but patronising grin on her before depositing two croissants on the plates at both table settings.

'*Jye!* I told you I don't want breakfast.'

'I know. But, like Flo always said, breakfast is the most important meal of the day. And I swear one bite of these will change your mind.'

Much more of his mother-hen routine and she was going to *lose* her mind, not to mention her rapidly deteriorating temper!

'Okay, so do you want a pot of tea or one of these fancy tea bags?'

'Jye!' She grabbed his arm to get his attention. 'I don't want tea or decaf or mind-altering pastries. I just want *coffee*. C-O-F-F-E-E. Okay?'

'No way, Steff—'

'*Excuse me?*'

'Caffeine isn't good for the baby, so—'

'Isn't goo— Oh, for God's sake! *I'm not pregnant!*' she roared, clutching her hair to prevent her throttling him with frustration.

'We don't know that for sure,' he responded calmly. 'And until we do, it's best not to take any chances. I thought about this a lot last night, and while we're both obviously *hoping* for the best we have to prepare for the worst. Just because neither of us planned this, it doesn't negate our responsibilities; which is why if you are pregnant we'll get married straight away.

'By the way,' he went on, pouring boiling water into her teapot, 'I was talking to a lawyer friend last night, and apparently there's a four-week legal "cooling off" period between applying for a licence and getting married. The good news is that it can be waived under certain conditions, and

I'm fairly certain Duncan will know someone with the clout to put in a good word for us and speed things along.'

'Jye…are you on medication?'

He frowned. 'No, why? Oh! I get it,' he said, looking miraculously enlightened. 'You're wondering whether there's the possibility of drugs affecting my sperm. Relax, no worries. Although I could probably have some kind of test if you're really concerned.'

*Oh, she was concerned all right!* Concerned that even the most *minuscule* possibility that he might have to surrender his single lifestyle had sent him completely round the twist! When she'd done the number on him about how the condom which hadn't been able to match their passion might have caused her to get pregnant, she'd only wanted to put the wind up him a bit, as a payback for his being so cavalier with her feelings while making her fall in love with him. She hadn't intended to turn him into a candidate for a padded cell. Of course if he continued at this rate until her period came, chances were he'd get his own payback by driving her crazy as well!

When they walked into Duncan's office he greeted them with unabashed delight.

'Well done! Well done!' he said, taking Jye's hand in both of his own and pumping it fiercely. Then he turned to Stephanie and embraced her in a manner usually reserved for birthdays and Christmas, soundly kissing her cheek.

Jye had never doubted Duncan Porter's fondness for either him or Stephanie, but demonstrations of it had always been few and far between. Which could only mean their guardian, like him, had never realised how much pleasure Stephanie received from tangible affection. But Jye realised it now because it was right there in her eyes and her smile, lighting up her whole face in a way that warmed him clear to his soul. At this moment she looked more beautiful than any woman he'd ever seen, and he wanted to trade places with Duncan and hold her more desperately than he would have believed possible. Though the original thought had emerged on a purely spiritual level, it wasn't long before the memory of how she'd responded to him on a physical level generated a rush of primal heat within him which mushroomed into a breath-defying excitement at the prospect of her carrying his child in her belly.

His child. Their child. A tiny little person that the two of them alone had created…

The feelings the concept produced within him, both mentally and physically, were beyond description, beyond his understanding. But one thing he *did* know was that Stephanie Elizabeth Bernadette Worthington could argue all she wanted about how a *real* marriage could only exist if it was based on love, and that she'd *never* marry anyone for anything less, but it would do her no good. *If she was carrying his child, she was also going to be wearing his ring!*

If she wanted to embrace the fanciful ideology of love, then fine. Jye had never believed in it and wasn't about to change his mind, but he couldn't deny that the thought of sharing a bed and *embracing her* every night for the rest of his life was rapidly undermining his aversion to matrimony. Not that he *wanted* her to be pregnant, of course! But if she was…

'Well, come on, Jye!' the old man chided, jolting him from his erotic daydreams. 'Sit down, and let's get on with discussing our latest acquisition,' he ordered, indicating the seat next to Stephanie's, before moving behind his desk and lowering himself into a high-backed executive chair with a pleased chuckle.

'You know, Jye, you're one hell of a negotiator. As you know, owning an island resort has always been my ultimate goal. But I can't begin to tell you what getting the Illusion Island complex means to me.'

'No need to,' Jye replied. 'The mile-wide grin pretty much says it all. But, like I said on the phone last night, I couldn't have managed it without Steff.'

A hint of pink rose in her cheeks and she shifted in her chair. 'He's exaggerating, Duncan, I—'

'Not from what Mulligan told me,' Duncan cut in.

The alarmed look Stephanie shot Jye said it all…if Duncan

had said one wrong word the whole venture could be down the tubes.

*'You've spoken with Mulligan?'* Jye asked, hoping that both he and Steff were merely sharing a hallucination.

'Yes, he called late last night, not long after you rang me. He sounded like he was three sheets to the wind to me, but then the old boy's rumoured to be as fond of the drink as he is women. Anyway,' he continued, 'apparently he's coming to Sydney in a few days and he wants us all to get together socially.'

*'Oh, God.'* Stephanie's soft gasp of despair mirrored Jye's feelings.

'So naturally I agree…' Duncan's words trailed off as he sent a concerned glance from Jye to a now ashen-faced Stephanie and back again. 'What's the matter?' he asked, his tone cautious, his eyes sharp. 'Is there some problem or hitch with this deal I'm not going to like?'

*'Hitch* is a particularly apt choice of word, don't you think, Steff?' Jye said wryly, earning himself a pained look.

'Come on, you pair, knock off the furtive looks and answer me,' the older man insisted. 'It's obvious there's something going on that I don't know about. Now what is it?'

*'That,'* Jye said, 'would probably be our marriage.'

While Duncan's initial reaction to learning of their charade had been a mix of disbelief and rank amusement, he hadn't been about to let a little thing like the absolute truth sour a brilliant deal; therefore it had been agreed that the charade marriage would have to be reactivated for the duration of the Mulligans' visit. However, while Duncan was willing to backup the story, he'd washed his hands of the finer details it would involve.

'I'm *not* moving into your apartment, Jye,' Stephanie told him over the Chinese meal he'd turned up with at her place that night.

'But my place is more convenient, and more in keeping with where a professional, successful married couple would live.'

'Not if they're planning a family, they wouldn't. And you, remember, are the one who got me pregnant, an—' She blushed. 'Um…eh…I mean, you told Tory that I might be, and—'

'And *jinxed us*, I think is the term you previously used.'

'Well… anyway, what I— Jye, stop looking at me like that!'

'Like what?'

'Like…like…like you're trying to see inside me or something…'

'I'm curious…'

Her perfectly arched brows veed to a frown. 'About what?'

'What do you think a child of ours would look like?'

She blinked. 'Jye…I'm not—'

'So you keep saying. But humour me, okay? I've never previously even thought about kids, but I keep getting these mental images of what ours would look like.' He frowned. 'Do you know if there are twins in your background by any chance?'

*'Twins! You're wishing twins on me?'*

'Of course not! It's just that one minute I picture a fat little blond-headed boy and the next a pixie-faced little girl with platinum curls. So I wondered—'

'I doubt they'd have blonde hair,' she said, too easily picturing a laughing, chubby toddler with hair as dark and glossy as the man opposite.

'Why not?' He grinned cheekily. 'I *know* yours is natural.'

'And yours is as black as your perverse sense of humour,' she retorted, knowing she was blushing, but hoping he'd think it was from anger or embarrassment rather than the heat his husky remark stirred deep in her belly.

He gave an unoffended laugh. 'Well, as quick as *your* wit is, my IQ is four points higher, so we probably should hope my intellect is dominant.'

'But only if it's compensated by my superior moral code, so it'll negate that four extra points of *intellect* that got us into this mess in the first place!

'Then again,' she added, 'it would serve you right to get a

daughter whose interest in sexual pursuits matched yours.' The look of absolute panic on his face made her chuckle. 'Oh, yeah, *that* would be priceless! You trying to control a daughter with your indiscriminate libido.'

'It won't happen,' he stated firmly. 'Because no daughter of mine would even be allowed to date until she was thirty.'

'Yeah? Well, I can assure you no daughter of *mine* will put up with that kind of dominated, protected, boring existence.'

'Oh, she won't be bored. There are a heap of things I could find to keep her occupied…like learning how to *cook*. Of course, under *those* circumstances—' he winked '—it'd be a big help if our son wanted to follow a career in firefighting.'

Stephanie struggled against the smile threatening to spread over her face. 'Don't you think juggling that *and* the chairmanship of Porter's might be a tad hectic for him?'

Jye showed genuine surprise. 'You'd really like to have a son go into the business?'

'Well, no…not unless he really wanted to,' she said. 'But I mean, it's no secret Duncan's earmarked you to take over from him eventually, and I figured you'd want to pass it on to your son.'

For a moment Jye lapsed into thoughtful silence. 'I've never really thought about it before, but I guess there is something cool about being able to pass on something as unique as Porter's to one's children. But I'm not a chauvinist, so it wouldn't matter if the child was a boy or a girl. Except that, like you said, they'd have to *want* to take it on.' he said. 'And I'd like to think I'd be just as supportive of my kid whether they wanted to follow in my footsteps or follow the professional surfing circuit.'

'That's exactly how I feel!' Stephanie endorsed. 'Parents are meant to gently guide and support, not push and restrict.'

'You think that's what Duncan did to us?'

'Not intentionally,' she said wryly. 'Let's face it, Duncan didn't have a clue what to do with us until we graduated from high school. If it hadn't been for Flo organising trips and excursions for him to take us on during our holidays, probably the only place we would have gone besides school would've been the office.'

Her words brought a concerned look to Jye's face. 'Are you saying you weren't happy growing up?'

'God, no, Jye! Of course not! I love Duncan, and I loved having him as a guardian. It's just that sometimes I feel like *he* missed out on a lot of the good stuff parents should have.'

'How so?'

'Well, he'd never anticipated being a parent, and then, when he did get landed with us, establishing and running Porter's had numbed all his parental instincts. To me, it always seemed he was so obsessed and worried about being a *responsible* guardian to us that he never relaxed enough to experience the joys merely being a good parent can be. I'm not saying *we* missed out on anything, but I think Godfather did, although he doesn't know it.'

Again her words left Jye silent and pondering for several seconds. Then, sighing, he leaned forward intently. 'Steff, I know you don't think I'm fit to be a good father, but—'

'I never said that!'

He shrugged, a rueful grimace tugging at his lips. 'Maybe not in so many words, but you've stated categorically you don't want to marry me.'

'Only because I know exactly how you feel about marriage!' she exclaimed. 'Geez, Jye, just because I doubt your ability as a husband doesn't mean I don't think you wouldn't be a good father to our child. Talk about half listening to what's said to you!' she huffed, secretly admitting that much of her irritation came from the guilt of knowing she'd unwittingly hurt his feelings.

He blinked. 'But you just said one of the problems Duncan faced was that he'd never anticipated being a parent,' he reminded her. 'And fatherhood has always been the furthest thing from my mind too; so therefore—'

'In the *past* it might've been the furthest thing from your mind,' she cut in. 'But you've done nothing but anticipate it for days! For heaven's sake, you've already started monitoring my diet and speculating on what our children will look like, and we don't even know for sure if I'm pregnant.'

Jye waited, fully expecting her to add that she was sure she *wasn't* pregnant, but surprisingly no such qualification came, and he couldn't quell the rush of pleasure its absence brought.

'So even though you reckon I'd be the equivalent to the anti-Christ as a husband, you really think I'd make a good parent, huh?'

A self-conscious smile played at her lips, but her eyes met his with sincerity as she nodded. 'Yeah, I think you'll be a good father.' The smile widened to a cheeky grin. 'You might be a womaniser, but I'm pretty sure that's not a scientifically proven genetic trait, so our son would be spared in that regard. Apart from that, basically you're a good person.'

'And basically you're a brat, but—'

'I am *not*,' she lied, with true indignation, 'and never have been a brat.'

He laughed. 'Yeah, you are,' he corrected. 'In the past you were just cute enough to get away with it.' Reaching across the table, he drew a lazy finger along her cheekbone. 'Now you're more than beautiful enough to get away with it.' His thumb grazed her lip, sending her bloodstream manic. 'Tell me…are seductive almond-shaped blue eyes dominant over uninspired brown, or vice versa?'

'Your eyes aren't uninspired brown,' she whispered. 'They're black as coal.' It could only have been the last remnants of self-respect that propelled Stephanie to pull back at the very instant her malfunctioning brain had her beginning to turn her lips into Jye's palm.

'Black as coal, huh?' His voice was rank with amusement. 'I'll have to get my passport details changed.'

Feeling like the biggest fool on God's earth, as much for what she'd said as what she'd almost done, she frantically began clearing the table. Annoyingly, he stood and started to assist her. Of course the quiet, efficient way he stacked the dishes was a blatant contrast to the chinking and cluttering her trembling hands produced. Her uneasiness was further magnified when, even without looking up, she sensed his gaze fixed solely and intently on her, and her lovesick mind began imagining she could feel him caressing her non-existent breasts. When her nipples hardened in response she literally bolted into the kitchen.

'So what's dominant?' he persisted, following her. 'Blue-grey or coal-black?'

She spun around, surprised not by the teasing mockery in the reference to his eye colouring but the description of hers. No one but Flo, their former housekeeper, had ever noticed that her eyes tended to change colour, depending on her mood.

'Right now they're blue,' he said, reading her mind. 'But I bet I can turn them grey.' His focus was solely on her face, and seared her all the way to her bones. Bones already weakened by his nearness and the soft laziness of his voice.

'I...I wouldn't advise it,' she muttered, taking the dishes he held and hastily turning to make a production of piling them in the sink.

'Why?'

She swallowed hard and tried to muster sarcasm. 'Because after the mess you've got us into with the Mulligans, get me mad now and chances are I'll be the only one left breathing in the room.'

It was the ultimate in bravado, since her voice came out as if she hadn't drawn a breath for years. Then his denim-clad thighs pressed against the back of her bare ones and her lungs, along with every other vital organ, teetered on complete breakdown.

'What makes you think I want to get you mad?' His breath on her neck suddenly seemed more sense-destroying than the warm weight of his body against her.

'Because...um...Flo says that when I'm furious my eyes turn to smoke.' *Oh, dear Lord,* she thought frantically. *If this is a test for sainthood, I gotta tell you I'm going to fail miserably.*

'Yeah, well, Flo doesn't know everything...' His mouth finally made contact with the flesh of her neck, sending shivers of temptation and delight along her spine. Large, masculine hands settled over hers where they fiercely gripped the sink. 'Desire and passion turn them a beautiful soft grey too… Steff…' he whispered as she felt the length of his body stiffen against hers. 'Say no and I stop, *now*.'

A light ironic laugh bubbled from her lips a moment before she said, 'Then, *yes. Yes. Yes. Yes. Yes.*'

He turned her to him then, or perhaps she turned of her own accord, but the end result was that she was wedged between the safe, solid hardness of the sink and the dangerous masculine hardness of Jye. Except that once again his obvious passion was softened with tenderness.

'You're gorgeous, you know that?' His hands stroked up over her shoulders, then her neck, to anchor at the base of her skull, and his thumbs began brushing her ears. Then slowly, *oh, so slowly*, he lowered his head to feather his lips across hers. Once. Twice. Three times.

By the time he slid his hands over her buttocks and lifted her against him, Stephanie's heart was floating somewhere above her head, her brain was long past its use-by date, and the option of *not* wrapping her legs tightly around him was one she didn't want to take.

What she did want to take was the opportunity of again being Jye's lover, no matter how temporarily she would have that role. Lifting her fingers, she began lazily tracing the fascinating ridges and planes of his handsome face.

'So tell me,' she said, her voice husky from passion as well as nerves. 'Are we about to have another one-night stand, or have you changed your mind about us having an affair?'

His expression as he studied her face was so reverent Stephanie felt as if she was the most beautiful woman alive.

'Oh, honey,' he whispered hoarsely. 'I've changed my mind about a lot of things…'

# CHAPTER TWELVE

THEIR clothing was shed in passionate haste by eager, hungry hands, with only mutual mutterings of appreciation for each other's bodies and hot, greedy kisses slowing proceedings. But as one they fell onto Stephanie's bed, and the urgency of their desire gave way to the sensual pleasure of an unhurried languid exploration of each other.

For Stephanie it was the most arousing yet spiritual experience of her life, and being able to caress Jye's bare, muscled flesh was suddenly the most erotic pleasure she could imagine. Feeling him rain butterfly kisses down her calves and along the soles of her feet created sensations so emotionally and physically stirring that she hovered between tears of joy and climactic fulfilment. *How could a man capable of such immense tenderness not believe in love?*

'Your skin's like liquid satin,' he breathed, his lips teasing a path from her thigh, across her groin and onward to her belly. 'I want to touch…and taste every millimetre of it…' He paused in the torment of his hot, wet kisses to raise his head and stare at her through desire-clouded eyes. 'Tell me what you want…what you like.'

That he should make such an inane request when her whole body, not to mention her heart, was next door to ecstasy made her smile. 'No point,' she said, sliding one hand through the silkiness of his hair and the other along the seductive roughness of his late-evening beard, her words little more than a blissful sigh. 'So far you seem to be reading my every thought before I even have it.'

'Tell me anyway,' he urged. 'I want to know what you like me doing.' Keeping his eyes on hers his laved his tongue around and into her navel as he rolled her nipples between her fingers.

161

'Every…thing,' she gasped, writhing from the scorching cravings building within her and fighting to hold back the words of love she dared not utter. There would never be a man who could fulfil her as Jye did, and the knowledge was as incredibly consoling as it was painful, because it made what she was experiencing now so much more special. But with his mouth and hands lifting her closer and closer to what she knew was as near to heaven as she'd get with a pulse, it became harder and harder to keep the chant of *I love you… I love you…* safely silent within her head.

Then suddenly all her fragile thoughts were banished, her whole body bucking in rapture as his fingers delved between her curls and his thumb began inwardly caressing her. For an indeterminately delicious time the bliss he was building her towards was all she craved…then instantly it *wasn't.*

'Jye!' she cried. 'Stop! Stop now!'

The shrill urgency of her voice stopped Jye's heart and halted his hand even before she grabbed his wrist. Panic rose in his throat as fear and remorse knotted in his gut. 'Oh, hell, baby, what's wrong? Did I hurt—?'

Furiously shaking her head, she dragged him to where she could take possession of his mouth. The fervour of her short, hungry kiss dispersed any anxiety that he'd inadvertently caused her pain; it also turned him inside out and shredded every nerve in his body.

'Ah, Steff… Geez, honey, don't scare me like that. I thought I'd hurt you, or done something you didn't like.'

'Oh, Jye…I love everything you do to me. But this time I want you to come *with* me. *In* me. *Now.*'

The sheer emotiveness of her words and the feel of her hand closing around him sent him right to the edge; in fact his last semi-conscious thought, as Steff deftly sheathed him with a condom, was how the hell could her common sense possibly still be functioning at a time like this? The only thing his mind or body could process was their all-consuming need to possess her.

\* \* \*

Her damp head rested in the crook of his equally sweaty arm, her legs were entwined with his, and in the dimly lit room her lungs sucked in air with the same needy rhythm as his own—yet Jye doubted they shared the same thoughts... He'd credited the sheer unequalled brilliance of their union on Illusion Island to a waterbed, so how the hell did he reconcile his theory with the fact that now, as he lay in a state of complete sexual satiation, the only thing beneath him was a regular inner-sprung mattress?

'Jye...' Her breath dusted his skin.

'Mmm.'

'This is probably going to sound trite and naive to you...' The hesitancy in her voice was mirrored in the way her fingers played nervously over his chest. 'But...well, I want you to know that making love with you is better than it's ever been with anyone else. Better than I imagined it could be.'

Feeling her stiffen at his burst of wry laughter, Jye instinctively tightened his hold before embarrassment or indignation sent her leaping from the bed. 'Whoa, honey! I'm not laughing at *you*. You're right; it was pretty damned good.'

She jerked up to stare down at him. '*Pretty damned good?* Good?' The slow shake of her head and droll expression was as cute as it was amusing.

'Well, fine,' she went on, 'I suppose I'll have to bow to your superior knowledge and experience of what rates well in the bedroom, but, *sheesh*; if that's only *good*...boy, I've really gotta get out more!'

Despite the teasing light in her eyes, the comment didn't strike Jye as one bit funny, and in a single move he had her pinned beneath him. 'Oh, no, you won't! I think I should warn you that there are certain standards I expect the mother of my child to uphold.'

'Oh?' The amusement in her eyes faded. 'Well, the verdict isn't in on that yet.'

'Nevertheless, don't even think of leaving this *bed* any time soon, let alone *getting out more*. I'll concede that when

I said it was good between us I may have understated things a tad…' He grinned. 'But, since I've got the rest of the night free, if you're interested perhaps we could repeat the exercise and I'll reassess my earlier rating.'

'*The rest of the night?* You aren't going to go home?'

'I wasn't planning to…' He frowned. 'Why? Do you want me to go home?'

'No, of course not,' she said quickly. 'It's just you've always made it your hard and fast rule *never* to spend a night with a lover, even if you were having an ongoing affair with them.'

'It's like I told you earlier, Steff; I'm changing my mind about a lot of things…'

Stephanie told herself not to take too much heart from his words, but it was hard advice to follow in the wake of his tender, attentive actions that night. And it got harder still in the days and nights which followed…

Every morning he rose to bring her a glass of juice and cup of decaf coffee in bed, and the knowledge that once she'd satisfied him by drinking both he in turn would satisfy her by helping her shower made Stephanie conclude giving up caffeine was even more stimulating than consuming it!

They'd disciplined themselves to abandoning the shower once the hot water ran out and dressing in unison before sharing a mirror so Jye could shave while she applied her make-up. Of course, since they both lacked the discipline to resist spontaneous kisses, which usually ended up engaging more than just their lips, they invariably had to rush like crazy to leave her house with enough time to stop off at the bakery so they could eat breakfast on the drive to the office.

If anyone at the Porter's headquarters noticed Jye now tended to pop into Stephanie's office several times a day instead of a couple of times a week, as had previously been his habit, no one commented. But beyond that they went out of their way not to advertise their changed relationship. Duncan naturally assumed they'd taken up his suggestion that Jye should stay over at Stephanie's as a precaution against the imminent but non-specified arrival of the Mulligans, and if the parking attendant was curious as to why they'd started arriving and departing the office together, he was too discreet to show it.

Stephanie knew her life was as perfect as it was ever going to get. She'd always known Jye wasn't into long-term commitment, and now she knew that, feeling as she did about him, marriage to anyone else in her future was impossible. It was when these depressing thoughts forced their way into her head that she often found her hand settling on her stomach and a chant of, *But what if I am? There is a possibility*... echoing over and over in her heart, until fledgling hopes began elevating her spirits again.

It wasn't that she wanted to trap Jye into marriage, she told herself, when on the fifth day of their 'affair', after a weekend when the only time they'd left her bed was to drive to Jye's apartment, check out *his* bed and collect some clothes for him, she again caught herself thinking, *But what if...?*

No, she could never steal Jye's freedom, but the thought of having his child filled her with an unparalleled joy. For, while she'd never be able to teach Jye that love existed, it was a lesson she knew a child of hers would learn well.

It was only three days to her period. She'd always been so regular she could practically pick the hour it would arrive...*but what if it didn't...?*

Going by dates, she should have been relatively safe the night one solitary condom had malfunctioned. But *should have been safe* wasn't the same as *definitely was safe*...

'Deep in thought, Stephanie?'

'Oh! Duncan...eh, hi.' She shuffled the folders on her desk in the hope of looking vaguely efficient. 'What can I do for you?'

'I popped in to let you know Brad Carey is back on deck.'

She schooled her face to only mild interest. 'Oh, that's right...he's been on his honeymoon.'

'Well, that too, but he's also been doing a little…shall we say, *undercover work* on Illusion Island for me.'

*Duncan knew Brad had been at the Illusion Resort?*

'As our senior architect, I wanted him to get a first-hand look at the layout of the place so we can get a jump start on planning what changes we're going to make. I decided since he was going to miss work because of his honeymoon it was to our advantage to kill two birds with one stone; good deal for him too, since he got a free honeymoon out of it.'

Stephanie struggled to collate the information she was getting. 'And, er…Jye knew Brad was going to be at the resort?'

'No. However, I especially warned Carey not to be surprised if he saw Jye there, but to avoid him at all cost—'

*Oh, great! They'd sweated blood avoiding him, and all the while he'd been avoiding them!*

'I couldn't take the chance of old Mulligan getting wind that Carey was a Porter employee and guessing how interested I was in things. Damn clever bit of industrial espionage, if I do say so myself.' He chuckled smugly, then said, 'Anyway, I want you to pop down and take a look at what Carey's come up with some time over the next couple of days. As Head of Promotions, and since you've seen the set-up as it stands, I want you to have some input on what we need to offer our guests to stay ahead of the competition.'

'Of course. Um, Duncan, I'm curious… You've always been so dead set against inter-office relationships; so how come you haven't transferred Karrie Dent now she and Brad have married?'

'Purely because they strike me as not being the type of people to allow their personal relationship to encroach on their work. Both of them are sufficiently ambitious not to waste time necking in corridors or copulating on desks in their lunch hour,' he said frankly.

'I've always prided myself on being a fair man, Stephanie; if people have the drive and ambition to keep their professional and private lives distinctly separate during business hours then I don't have a problem with them having a personal relationship in their own time. It's when personal emotions invade the office and work priorities are put at risk that efficiency suffers.'

Jye chuckled when Stephanie relayed the story to him after he arrived in her office with lunch a couple of hours later.

'So why *didn't* you mention to Duncan that we'd seen Brad holidaying at a rival resort?' she asked around the straw of the chocolate milkshake Jye had presented to her with the announcement she needed to drink more milk.

'I planned to tackle Carey about it myself.' *Along with a few other things, namely, staying the hell away from Stephanie in the future if he wanted to keep his teeth not to mention his job.*

'So,' he said. 'Did the old man say whether he'd heard any more from Mulligan?'

'No, thank goodness.' She sighed. 'It was one thing to go with our instincts in a moment of crisis in the relative safety and isolation of Illusions, but I feel really devious carrying on the charade now we're back in the real world. If you follow what I mean…'

'I think I do,' he said, moving to gently tug her out of her chair. 'You were comfortable when it was only you and me, but everything seems that much more out of control having someone else involved—even Duncan.'

'Especially Duncan,' she qualified. 'I know confession would undoubtedly be good for *my* soul, but I also know fessing up now would not only screw the deal, it'd destroy the Porter Corporation's name. Either way we'd hurt Duncan, which makes the truth a no-win situation.'

The concern in her eyes made Jye wish he could regret thinking up the stunt in the first place, but the reality was that while he, too, was uneasy with Mulligan's imminent visit, there was no way he could regret the changes the ruse had brought about in his relationship with Stephanie.

'We'll get through it, Steff,' he promised. Then, threading his fingers through her riot of silver curls, added, 'It's probably not much consolation to you, but for what it's worth us being married feels less like a charade to me now than it did on the island.'

He didn't have a chance to analyse the admission, which startled even him, because he could no more have held back from kissing the soft 'O' of surprise from her mouth than he could have held back time. And as her arms closed around his waist, and her elegant curves knitted perfectly against him, he realised that with Stephanie he felt a personal completion he'd not even been aware he'd been lacking.

Drawing her as close as they could get, vertical and fully clothed, he deepened his kiss in a bid to milk more of whatever magic she transferred to him. Frantic for the touch of her bare flesh, he tugged the back of her blouse from her skirt, but the instant gratification he received from her heated softness was short-lived, when her eager tongue and sleek, nibbling teeth responded to his desperation with a passion that only intensified it more. It took every milligram of self-discipline he possessed to eventually remove his hands and ease her away from him.

Her breathing was as ragged as his own, and the desire hazing her grey eyes had him mentally cursing their surroundings.

'Honey…if I don't get out of here now, I'm likely to break company policy and take you on the desk.'

'If you don't get out of here now, I'm likely to take you before we can even reach the desk.'

He groaned, her suggestiveness doing such crazy things to his insides that he didn't trust himself to even hold her as he bent and kissed her cheek. 'I'm outta here; though God knows how I'm going to be able to concentrate on anything for the rest of the afternoon…'

'Duncan's just spoken with Sir Frank,' Jye told her two days later, via an inter-office phone call. 'Apparently Tory is very insistent about wanting to have dinner with us.'

'With *you*, you mean,' Stephanie corrected. 'She hates my guts.'

The warm, masculine chuckle sent shivers of awareness down her spine even over the phone. 'If you want, I could get you out of it with a bout of morning sickness. By the way, did you know you can get that *any* time of day?'

Stephanie's eyes welled with tears. Last night Jye had buried his nose in a women's magazine he'd bought, which was running a special feature on pregnancy and childbirth. His deep interest in and constant recitation of various facts, figures and birthing techniques had nearly torn her heart out. Her period was due tomorrow, and all the signs were she *was* going to get it. Her breasts were fuller and more tender, and she was headachy and utterly miserable.

'Steff? Did you hear—'

'Jye, will you give it a rest?' she shouted. 'I'm *not* pregnant, okay?' She bit her lip against tears in the ensuing silence.

'You got your period.'

Expecting him either to take exception at the way she'd yelled or to tell her yet again she couldn't be certain of that, it took a moment for her to comprehend the flatly delivered statement.

'Eh…no, not yet. But trust me, it'll arrive on schedule tomorrow. I've had enough of them to recognise all the preliminary signs.' Blinking back tears, she forced a laugh for fear he'd pick up on her disappointment. 'One being my moodiness. I'm sorry, Jye, I didn't mean to jump down your thro—'

'*Tomorrow?* But you told me it was due today.'

The accusing tone grated on her. He might have been all gungho about preparing for the worst, but it had been all show and no substance. She couldn't withhold her sarcasm.

'I meant I'd get it *by* tomorrow morning, but if you can't wait that long I'll set my alarm to go off every hour on the hour tonight, just so you don't have to endure the agony of suspense longer than absolutely necessary!

'Now, about this thing with the Mulligans,' she went on

quickly, desperate to end the call before she lost it completely. 'I'm not going to bail out on you, so go ahead and arrange whatever works for you and Duncan regarding dinner. Okay?'

'Steff, I—'

'Look, I've got to go. Eh…I told Duncan I'd look over some plans Brad's done. Catch you later,' she said, with a cheerfulness she wasn't sure worked through gritted teeth, and promptly hung up to dart from her office.

It took her a good fifteen minutes in the executive bathroom to compose herself and repair her make-up. She knew she was acting like an idiot. She'd known all along she wasn't pregnant. Yet somehow their fake marriage, his endearing interest in pregnancy and his constant rebuttals of her claims that she definitely *wasn't* having a baby, along with the sheer joy of waking each day alongside the man she loved, had allowed her dreams to become transposed with reality.

A sadly ironic laugh/sob broke from her. Falling in love on Illusion Island had actually made her so *de*lusional that on some deep, pathetic level, she'd almost allowed herself to believe she *was* married to Jye; she had begun to wish she *was* going to have his child, and even started hoping that just maybe their 'affair' could last the rest of her life—

She stopped mid-stride. Dear God, what was the matter with her? Okay, so she *wasn't* pregnant, and there was no need for Jye to have to marry her now, but that didn't mean she had to write off their relationship already. Talk about using a chainsaw to trim a split fingernail! Not being pregnant didn't mean she loved him less. It didn't mean that they couldn't still be lovers.

Oh, sure, her days with him were undoubtedly numbered, but Jye meant more to her than anything else in the world, and, damn it! she thought, striding confidently into the corridor, she *wasn't* going to burn her bridges prematurely. She'd learn how to enjoy the moment and she wasn't going to spoil what time she did have left with him by mourning the end of their relationship in advance. When it happened, she'd be prepared for it, but she was *not* going to give up on her happiness until *Jye told her* their relationship was over!

Of course, given the expression on his face as he came striding down the corridor towards her, it could mean her positive attitude was going to be extremely short-lived.

'Where have you been? I've searched all over the building for you!'

Taking some solace from first-hand knowledge that guys usually spoke gently in the lead-up to dumping you, she bit the bullet and asked, 'Why?'

'Because you said you had to go down to see Carey. That was *twenty minutes ago.*'

Call it women's intuition, or just plain old wishful thinking, but she didn't think jealousy from someone as self-confident as Jye indicated a loss of interest.

'Sorry,' she said, not feeling anything but elated by his uncharacteristic behaviour. 'The trip to the bathroom was an impulsive act. I'll try to remember to inform you of my precise actions and not...' she grinned '...*pee* so long in future.'

'Don't be cute! I've been worried sick.' Jye silently cursed himself for the admission. In actual fact he'd been relieved when Carey had initially said he hadn't seen her; he'd only started worrying when no one else in the building had either.

'You were worried about my seeing Brad?' Her expression was one of outright amusement, but the touch of her fingers against his cheek was as softly conciliatory as her next words. 'Oh, Jye...do you honestly think that after everything we've shared I could still be interested in him?'

'You damned well better not be!' he said gruffly, then hauled her against him when she had the audacity to laugh. 'What's so funny?'

She tilted her head mischievously. 'You mean besides the idea of you being jealous of Brad?'

'I never said I was jealous of him,' he pointed out, which

was the only response to spare him having to either lie or admit that for the first time in his life he felt threatened by another man. 'As a matter of fact, I was looking for you because I've come up with an idea of how we can avoid the Mulligans...' He remained silent way beyond her expression of intense interest, initially to tease her but then simply because looking at her made him feel so damn good—certainly a hell of a lot better than he'd felt after speaking to her on the phone.

He'd been worried that, despite her ongoing assurances she wasn't pregnant, on a subliminal level her long-held and often aired desire to experience motherhood might have left her vulnerable to actually having those assurances confirmed. And that then, in a fit of the endearing, albeit incomprehensible way she had of reasoning things out, she'd perhaps decide their relationship had run its term. It was while he'd been paralysed to the soul by the despair that thought had rendered that he'd been struck by a way to avert the situation.

'*Jye...*' She tugged his tie. '*Tell me what this great idea of yours is.*'

'Kiss me first.'

She grinned. 'Payment in advance? I think not, Mr Fox; let's hear how good it is first.'

'It's simple, but ingenious. Which leads me to think I should up your show of appreciation to two kisses...'

'*Jye!*'

'Okay... We take our vacations now.' Her statue-still astonishment made it easy to start backing her out of the centre of the corridor to the wall, where she continued to simply stare at him. Her curls, as always by this time of day, were as tussled and tempting as they were when she first woke, or after he'd driven his fingers through them during a bout of the exquisite lovemaking she'd brought into his life.

'Jye, be honest... Have you spent the afternoon sniffing glue?'

Chuckling, he nuzzled her neck. 'Why would I, when the scent of you creates the most potent high in the universe?'

'I can't believe this,' she muttered.

'It's true you smell great,' he teased, but instead of smiling Steff was staring at him as if he'd grown a second head.

'*You,*' she said, tapping his chest with a slim russet-tipped fingernail, 'Jye Fox, who's not taken more than a half-day off in…well, God knows how many years, are seriously suggesting we drop everything at a crucial time like this to take a vacation just…' she snapped her fingers '…like that?'

'Sure am. We're both overdue for one. And since we've already told Sir Frank we'd been apart for weeks prior to your arrival at the resort, it'll seem a perfectly legitimate explanation for our absence.'

She eyed him suspiciously, a faint smile hovering at her mouth. 'Are you sure you haven't fallen victim to something that featured in a recent episode of the *X Files*?'

'The only thing I've fallen victim to is you,' he said, cupping her face. 'Now quit being cute and admit it's a great plan.'

Her gorgeous gloss-slick mouth tightened in pensive silence, tempting Jye to kiss it back to its usual sexy softness. He was lowering his head as she spoke.

'What did Duncan say about this?'

He shrugged and kissed one corner of her mouth. 'I'll tell him when he gets back to the office,' he murmured against the second corner. 'I thought we could go to the house at the bay, where we don't have to do anything but move between the beach and the bedroom.'

He felt her soundless laughter. 'Does that mean you're giving up feeding me?'

'We'll order in pizza,' he murmured, moving his attentions to her neck. Her body squirmed in approval, which was all the encouragement he needed to step forward, sandwich her with his body against the wall and capture her breathy gasp with his mouth. Her response was swift and potent, and he cursed the fact the heat of her hands on his waist was insulated by his shirt.

'Um…er…I don't think Duncan will approve,' she said, once he reverted to nibbling on her throat.

'Yeah, he will. He knows the less contact we have with the Mulligans the better off—' He broke off when she pulled his head up to face her. Her eyes were dancing with amusement.

'I meant about us wasting company time and necking in the corridor.'

'Oh, right. And he's got a thing about copulating on desks too, hasn't he?'

She nodded.

'How do you think he'd be about touchy-feely in the stationery supply room?' he asked with comic speculation.

'About as thrilled as he'll be if we suddenly tell him we're leaving him to deal with the Mulligans on his own,' she said sagely. Reading Jye's intended protest in his face, she cut it off. 'Anyway, Jye, I can't manage a vacation right now. I've got work backed up into the next decade.'

It wasn't entirely a lie, Stephanie told herself. She did have a backlog of work because of having spent so much time out of the office the last few months. But the real reason she didn't want to use any of her vacation time was because she was saving it for that rainy day she knew was going to come. The day when Jye ended their relationship. Because when that happened there was no way she'd be able to continue working with him without a mourning period. Although deep down she knew her heart would never recover.

Pushing the thought aside, she forced a bright smile. 'Jye, stop worrying. Trust me, we'll get through tonight and that'll be the end of it all.'

# CHAPTER THIRTEEN

ALL night only one thought occupied Jye's mind: *I don't want this to be the end of it.*

It was only because he wore a watch that he knew dinner with the Mulligans and driving them to the airport to catch their private plane home had taken just on six hours; beyond that he couldn't have said what had happened during the evening. If he'd contributed anything in the way of intelligent conversation during that time it could only have been an impulsive response, because all he'd been aware of was Stephanie, the melodious tones of her voice and laughter. The heart-stopping beauty of her face had held him spellbound...

Yet now he was afraid to take his eyes from the road to steal even a glance at her for fear of prompting her into speech. Her complete and absolute silence since they'd farewelled the Mulligans had an ominous quality.

Turning the car into her street, he was again overwhelmed by an emotive dread he didn't understand. Or rather, it wasn't so much that he didn't understand it...he was just having a hard time accepting it. He needed time to think things through without distractions...time alone. Yet for the first time in his life the idea of being alone had him almost rigid with terror. The knowledge that today had become yesterday an hour and forty-two minutes ago, and consequently didn't give him a lot of time to sort himself out, wasn't a calming influence either.

On one level it seemed ludicrous that Steff would end things because she turned out *not* to be pregnant, when all along she'd refused to accept the possibility she was; surely she'd let their relationship evolve because she *wanted* it to, not because she believed it was inevitable they'd have to marry. But what if she decided that all bets were off now

175

that the worry of the Mulligans and parenthood were both going to be out of the way?

Prior to her rejecting his vacation idea, Jye had been convinced that if they got away from the shadows of Porter's and the Mulligan deal she'd realise that what they shared went beyond business and great sex. That it was…well, *special* in some way. But what chance did he have of explaining his feelings to her when he couldn't comprehend them himself?

Confusion was still his keeper when he swung into Stephanie's driveway, and the explosive brightness of the sensor light above the garage only made him feel more in the dark. And—

'Jye, I know Duncan will be expecting you back at your apartment, so there's no need for you to see me in.' Stephanie had her seatbelt off and was halfway out of the door before the car stopped rocking from the force with which he'd hit the brakes.

The smile she gave was so brittle that the only thing reassuring about it was that it meant his expression couldn't be as comically nonplussed as he felt. But even if he hadn't been momentarily speechless he doubted he'd have got a word in before she said, 'And you can tell Godfather for me that I wasn't amused with the underhanded way he dumped the trial of driving them to the airport onto us. *"My surgeon has advised me to be in bed by midnight at the latest"*,' she mimicked. 'Huh! Since when does an ingrown toenail count as surgery?'

By the time Jye got out of the car she was already crossing the lawn to the house, her voice still pitched vaguely towards him and her words going at a hundred miles an hour. 'Mind you, I'm not nearly as furious with him as I was at the time. It's such a damn relief to know the Mulligans are out of our hair once and for all. Call me a bitch,' she invited at her door, all her attention on rooting through the small evening purse she carried, 'but I'll bet the extended trip they're taking to Switzerland is a clinic camp for both of them. Alcohol rehab for him and more fantastic plastic for dear Tor— Oh, thank goodness!' She laughed, jiggling her keys. 'For a second I thought I'd be climbing in the window and having to explain myself to the police.'

'*Why?*' he asked tightly, her manic chatter having propelled his confusion past frustration into anger. 'Did you have the locks changed while I went home to pick up my dinner suit?'

Her laugh came a split second too late to ring entirely true. 'I guess it takes longer than a week to get used to sharing; I forgot I'd given you a key.'

Despite the dread of her answer, he forced himself to ask, 'Is that an oblique way of asking for it back?'

'No! No of course not!' He physically sagged with relief at her genuine look of distress.

'Okay. Then *why*,' he asked, tilting her chin, 'are you acting so damned anxious and in such a rush to get rid of me?'

As soon as he asked the question a light went on in his head. *Geez!* he thought. *I'm getting to be a bigger and bigger fool with every heartbeat.*

'Forget I asked that,' he murmured against her forehead. 'After my adolescent display of hormonal behaviour in the corridor today you're entitled to think I'd be insensitive enough to jump your bones whether you felt up to it or not,' he told her softly.

'It's not that,' she said quickly. 'It's just that with Duncan staying at your place he'll wonder what took you so long. And…and, well, I'd rather—'

'Not advertise the fact we're lovers?' he offered tightly.

She dropped her gaze.

The wordless action was not only loud and excruciatingly painful, but it prodded the marginal control he currently had on his temper. Knowing that if he opened his mouth now he'd undoubtedly say something he'd regret, he silently took the key from her fingers and opened the front door. Stepping into the hallway, he flicked on the light, then opened the hall cupboard and deactivated her alarm system.

The simple task was made difficult by his less than steady fingers on the keypad, but the extra second gave him a chance to convince himself he was reading way too much into her desire to keep their relationship a secret for a little longer. By her own admission, she was moody prior to her period.

He took a calming breath before tugging her into his arms for a thorough, but too brief kiss, and he was really gambling heavily on his will-power when he stole a longer one at the door which elicited little moans from deep in her throat.

'Night, honey,' he said. 'Be sure and lock the door behind me, okay?' She nodded, her eyes and face tight with the fatigue of a gruelling nineteen-hour day. 'And listen, don't bother setting your alarm clock,' he told her. 'I'll wake you with breakfast in bed.'

'No, don't! It'll be best if we go in separately tomorrow.' Another forced smile flashed over her face. 'Duncan, remember?'

Jye didn't bother reminding her that Duncan habitually headed into the office at the crack of dawn even when he didn't have to make the ninety-minute-plus trip from his semi-rural home. Nor did he demand to know why, within seconds of melting in his arms, she'd iced up again at the speed of light because he had a feeling he mightn't like her answer. Instead he nodded agreement, then walked to his car and backed out of her drive, more muddled than he'd been driving in.

It was a good thing the route to his apartment was so familiar he didn't have to think about it, because concern about where Steff and he were headed consumed all his attention.

Concern switched to dread next morning, when he learned that Steff had phoned her secretary instructing her to reschedule her appointments because she was 'off colour' and wouldn't be in.

When neither she nor her answering machine picked up

on his call, Jye bolted for his car, his nerves and gut tight with dread.

He managed the forty-minute journey in thirty-two, panic evidently being a speed-inducing negative emotion. But, unlike the last two occasions he'd negotiated her drive, this time he was swinging into it with screeching tyres and blessed with complete clarity of mind and an acceptance of all which for days had been churning through his head and his heart.

Scant minutes later the churning was relocated to his gut...the house was empty.


Ellee's eyes were nearly as wide as her gaping mouth as she stared back at Stephanie. *'What did you say?'*

'I slept with Jye,' she repeated.

'Holy cow! My God, Steff...*when*?'

'Several times.'

'Holy, holy cow! I... Eh...' She shook her head. 'Exactly how many times is "several"?'

She shrugged. 'A lot. We're, eh...having an affair.'

*'You're* having an affair!' Ellee's shock was reflected in the faces of the surrounding patrons of the upmarket café in the foyer of the hotel Ellee managed. Belatedly she lowered her tone, to deliver another hushed, but still bemused, 'I can't believe it, Steff... I mean, holy cow! An affair...and with *Jye*, of all people.'

'Believe it. We've been living together for—'

'Living to— Hol—'

'It gets worse,' she cut in, before Elle made it necessary for the Vatican to employ stockmen. 'I've fallen in love with him.'

Elle waved a dismissing hand. 'Well, I worked that out. You've never slept with a guy you haven't been in love with.'

'Yeah, and I've never slept with a guy and *prayed* I'd be pregnant.'

*'You're going to have Jye's baby?'*

Stephanie wished the question didn't hurt so much. 'If

only... The only thing I want more than that is him. Exce...except I know I'm not going to end up w-w-with *either*!' And for the twelve-hundredth time that morning she burst into tears.

After wasting three hours of Porter Corporation time by keeping Ellee from her duties and telling her the whole sorry story, Stephanie knew it was time to get a grip. And, as she always did when she was miserable, or a romance started crumbling around her ears, she decided to go shopping.

Since buying the sofa hadn't immediately solved the pain of losing Brad, when she'd only *imagined* herself in love with him, furniture sure wouldn't help when it came to Jye. She wanted something more personal, like a necklace or a ring, perhaps—no, *not* a ring! *Definitely not a ring*, she resolved, struggling yet again to keep tears at bay.

Rings would bring back memories of what Jye had said on Illusion Island, when she'd asked him to pick out a ring for her to wear. She didn't need reminders of how surprisingly romantic and sensitive he could be; she needed something to remind her and convince her she *was* better off without him. Cooking! *That* was it! Jye was always insulting her culinary skills and her desire to cook... She'd buy some recipe books and food and all the state-of-the-art cooking equipment necessary to turn her into a genius in the kitchen! And then she'd make Jye *eat his words*!

Four hours and thousands of dollars later, Stephanie was miserable to the point of physical pain. All she'd succeeded in doing was proving that when you loved someone with all your heart and soul, and that love wasn't reciprocated, all the shopping, peeling, chopping and slicing in the world didn't have a hope of blocking the hurt from either your brain or heart even temporarily.

She tried telling herself that all wasn't yet lost, but 'herself' wouldn't buy the story. Not even to the point where she could muster sufficient pseudo-enthusiasm to transfer the mountains of prepared vegetables, meat and fish into her new wok, or even unpack the antique Royal Doulton dinner set she'd bought to go with her sparkling new sterling silver cutlery.

With luck this third cup of chamomile tea might help her get through tonight without her falling apart in front of Jye. Although after a day of almost non-stop crying, and an abundance of sympathy from Ellee and countless sales assistants, Stephanie figured she ought to be safely past the stage of tears if not entirely cried dry. So, realistically, her spirits probably had nowhere else to go but up. Who knew? Maybe in a day or two, when her dining room setting was delivered, she'd be in a better mood to appreciate things and could throw a dinner party to mark the start of her childless, single, loveless future?

The sound of Jye's car caused her heart to start pounding, even though she'd been watching the clock since Ellee's warning call. This was it. The beginning of the inevitable end.

*Oh, God, please let the end take a real long, long time to come,* she prayed, remaining curled on the sofa, counting the number of beats her heart made until he walked into the room.

'Why didn't you call me and tell me?' he asked.

No *Hello*, no *How are you feeling?* just an irritated demand. Stephanie cursed at the futile hope that had doggedly refused to leave her all day. In a bid to keep a check on her very limited composure, she continued to stare out of the window. 'I didn't see any point in worrying you until I knew for sure there was a reason.'

'*Really?* Well, did it ever occur to you I might've been even more worried when you didn't turn up for work? When there was no answer to my calls? When I drove here this morning and found you weren't here? Hell, Stephanie, if I hadn't finally tracked Ellee down at a business dinner my next stop was going to be the police.'

She remained with her back to him, rigidly immobile; Jye had never felt so frustrated nor effectively frozen out as he did at this minute. 'Damn it! Turn around and look at me, Stephanie!'

When she did her look of utter despair broke his heart. Her eyes, bloodshot and red-rimmed, looked the size of pizza trays in her pale, drawn face. Dear God, he'd never seen that beautiful face looking so unhappy so…so resignedly miserable.

'Oh, Steff—'

She leapt to her feet, out of his reach, the moment he moved to touch her. 'At the risk of offending you with an understatement, Jye, the bad news is that I *didn't* get my period last night. It still hasn't shown up. And, according to that magazine you bought, tender breasts and the other discomforts of premenstruation can also occur with pregnancy.'

'So you're pregnant.'

'I…I'm not sure. But you were the one who said we should be prepared for the worst.'

Yeah, he'd said that. Except now, hearing Stephanie echo the advice had an Arctic chill invading his veins.

'Well, then, I guess it's time to use that home pregnancy test kit I bought and find out for su—'

'*You* bought a test kit?'

He nodded. 'It's in the cabinet under the vanity. Eh, if you're ready… I'll go get it, and we can check out the instructions again and do the test now.'

'They're supposed to be done with an early-morning urine sample.'

'Oh. Then I supposed we'll have to wait until tomorrow mor—'

'No, we don't,' she corrected, then took a deep breath before adding, 'I bought a kit too, and I've already done the test.'

He frowned. 'But you said you didn't know—oh, you mean you're still waiting on the results?'

'No.' She sighed. 'I've been too scared to look. Trying to delude myself with the "no news is good news" theory. Or maybe the "ignorance is bliss" adage is more appropriate in this case,' she added bitterly.

Knowing one of them would have to summon the courage to stop dancing around the inevitable, he took a deep breath, held it, then released it. 'Okay... Where's the test? I'll check it.'

Instantly she pivoted. 'No. I'll come too.'

When she went to dart past him, he snared her hand and squeezed it tight. She gave a slightly hysterical laugh. 'How ironic! In childbirth it's the woman who does the squeezing.'

Bare seconds later, Jye stared at the small vial on Steff's dressing table. It was as far from blue as it could get. The instructions on the kit he'd bought stated, *'Blue result positive; unchanged negative'.*

With a plaintive cry, Stephanie pulled free of his hand. The abject despair on her face as she backed away from the dresser stabbed at his heart.

'Steff, it's okay,' he said quickly. 'It's clear. See?' He held it up as evidence. 'You're not pregnant. If you were it'd be blue.'

'I know that!' she snapped.

'You...you do? But...but you're *crying*—I don't understand.'

'Of course you don't! You've never wanted children, but I've wanted to be a mother for as long as I can remember,' she sobbed. *'I wanted this baby so much.'*

'Oh, honey, easy there... This doesn't mean you won't be able to have other children, *babies*, in the future. Hell, you're only twent—'

'But I don't want *other* children! I wanted this baby! Y-your baby. Our b-baby... Oh, God...I wanted it so much...'

Her words might have been mumbled around sobs, through tears and hiccuped gasps for air, but Jye heard them clearer than he'd ever heard anything. And the instant he did, hope started pumping his heart to such a size he expected his chest to burst.

'I wanted *your* baby.'

'Wh-why?' He could barely speak around the lump in his throat, but as hard as it was to talk he needed to *hear* her say those three words; then if he was struck deaf to-morrow he'd still be the happiest, most blessed man alive. 'Tell me why, Stephanie,' he urged again.

'Because...I'm in love with you, damn it! I know you won't believe that, that you think there's no such thing, but it *exists*, Jye,' she insisted, her face and voice urgent with conviction. 'When it happens, you know. I can't explain it, but—'

'Then let me try,' he cut in softly, trapping her wide-eyed gaze. 'Love exists when just hearing a person's name makes you turn around, hoping they'll be there. It's when just looking at them sends your pulse into a heavy metal rhythm, yet the sound of their voice is the most wonderful classical symphony you'll ever hear; it's having a person in your mind almost every minute that you're away from them and in every crevice of your heart continuously. Loving someone means their touch is both the most arous-ing and comforting thing you've ever experienced. It's ex-periencing the best sex of your life, but discovering your heart is the most erogenous zone in your whole body. It's not the safe, raw desire of sharing the ultimate physical closeness, but the rollercoaster of emotions that comes with feeling another person's pain and joy as strongly as if they were your own.

'But what makes real love...*real love*, Steff, so precious is that it's elusive. It can't be merely "found", no matter how desperately it's sought. Yet it can't be ignored indefi-nitely when it's right under a person's nose, no matter how stupidly or stubbornly that person wants to deny its exist-ence.

'I've believed in love ever since everything I *thought* I wanted turned out to be the exact opposite of what I needed to be happy, and I discovered a joy so intense I'm just not willing to go back to denying myself by denying love.

'I'll be the first to admit I've been incredibly stupid and stubborn, Stephanie...but I swear to God that I love you more than you'll ever know. And that I'll never stop lov-ing you.'

Her dizzy brain and tear-blurred eyes were incapable of estimating the distance separating them, but she blindly flung herself forward, trusting him to catch her. When he did, his mouth claimed hers with a passion that simultaneously swelled her heart and shrank her bones.

'Oh, God, Steff! I love you so much! So damned much! Please, please don't cry,' he begged, kissing the dampness from her cheeks. 'We'll get it right next time. I know it's disappointing that we aren't having a baby, but we can have a dozen kids if you want—' He broke off as she pulled back to stare at him, her brow etched into a frown above puzzled eyes surrounded by spiky wet lashes.

'Are you saying *you* were hoping I was pregnant too?' He nodded, his smile bittersweet. 'Since when?' she asked, her tone dazed.

'I'm not sure of the *exact* date,' he teased. 'But I do know that from the first time I imagined you with your belly swollen from a baby we created I realised there are worse things that could happen. And then one day,' he said softly, 'I realised that *not* seeing you pregnant with our child was one of them.'

The beauty and sincerity of his declaration left her feeling like the luckiest and most cherished woman on earth. 'Oh, Jye...' Hugging him tight, she rested her head on his chest. 'I've never thought anything would make me this happy.'

'Not even,' he said wryly, 'a huge, no expenses spared wedding?'

She jerked back. 'Jye Fox! Having your love and your children is much more important to me than marrying you.'

'*Excuse me?*' He looked so completely bewildered that Stephanie had to laugh.

'Oh, c'mon, Jye...I've always been aware of how you feel about marriage. But now that I know how you feel about me...well, marriage is quite irrelevant. It's not an issue any more,' she explained, 'because I *know* we're going to be together for the rest of our lives. I don't need a piece of paper signed in front of five hundred guests as security.'

'So you're saying we'll have kids, but you only want us to just…just live together?'

She nodded. 'Naturally the kids would have your name,' she added, before his expression hinted that perhaps she'd misinterpreted something he'd said. 'That *is* what you want, isn't it?'

'Hell, no! I want us married in the eyes of the law, the Church and our kids, and you wearing a ring big enough to let every damn male within a ten-mile radius know that you're off the market permanently!'

'You mean…you really *want* to marry me?' she asked, worried that perhaps euphoric joy might be affecting her hearing.

'Of course I want to marry you! Dear Lord, Stephanie, haven't you understood a word I've said? I *love* you. I want us to start a family. A *traditional* family. And I want us to have a traditional house with photographs of us in wedding regalia on our mantelpiece and stacks of photo albums for the kids to look at.

'The next time someone asks about our wedding day— and the kids *will* ask us—I want to be able to *have had one* so we'll keep our stories straight! And I want to be able to recall what it felt like to hold you in my arms during the bridal waltz, when we're both too old and arthritic to want to do anything but lie in bed. The—'

Laughing, she gagged him with her hand. 'Sheesh! Okay, okay. I'll marry you! And, while I can't ever imagine you being so old as to just want to *lie* in bed, I definitely think someone should be around to document such a monumental occurrence.'

'Well, you don't have to make it sound like you're humouring me,' he said, with mock poutiness. 'I'd like to think you had a good reason for accepting…'

She fought to keep her face as straight as his was. 'Oh, but I do!' Cupping his cheek, she produced her most seductive smile. 'Becoming Stephanie Elizabeth Bernadette

*Fox* is going to make me unbelievably happy for the rest of my life.'

He smiled. 'Now *that* sounded like you were being sincere.'

'I was. I'm going to truly enjoy being Mrs *Fox*. Because with thirty-nine letters in my name, cutting Worthington is gonna make filling out forms and writing cheques much fast— Eeikk!' she squealed as he swung her into his arms.

'You're incorrigible! You know that?' he said, tossing her laughing form onto the bed, then following her down onto the mattress.

'Now all I have to do,' he said, his fingers popping the first button on her blouse, 'is get you pregnant...'

As the dawn sun crept into the bedroom a thought leapt into Jye's head, prompting him to give up trying to figure out how accepting love could lift the union of two people beyond the realms of any verbal description and lurch into a sitting position.

'Jye... What's wrong?'

'It's possible you might be pregnant after all,' he said eagerly. 'I just remembered reading that sometimes early pregnancy tests can be wrong. Sometimes even early blood tests are wrong. I'll get the magazine—' A gentle hand on his arm stopped him before he made it out of the bed.

'Honey, I'm not pregnant.'

'But you can't be certain.'

Looking into his hopeful coal eyes, Stephanie knew she'd achieved dreams without equal.

'Yes, I can.' She smiled. 'As yet I mightn't have physical proof, but then I don't expect I'll need a test to tell me when I am either, because...' She touched her breast. 'I'll know in here. Loving you as much as I do, Jye, my heart will register the instant God blesses that love.'

And to Jye's amazement, four months later she was as good as her word, announcing he was going to be a father three weeks before even a doctor could confirm it...

# MILLS & BOON®

## *Makes any time special*

## Enjoy a romantic novel from
## *Mills & Boon*®

*Presents™   Enchanted™   Temptation*

*Historical Romance™   Medical Romance™*

# MILLS & BOON®

## Next Month's Romance Titles

♡

Each month you can choose from a wide variety of romance novels from Mills & Boon®. Below are the new titles to look out for next month from the Presents™ and Enchanted™ series.

## *Presents*™

| | |
|---|---|
| THE PERFECT LOVER | Penny Jordan |
| TO BE A HUSBAND | Carole Mortimer |
| THE BOSS'S BABY | Miranda Lee |
| ONE BRIDEGROOM REQUIRED! | Sharon Kendrick |
| THE SEXIEST MAN ALIVE | Sandra Marton |
| FORGOTTEN ENGAGEMENT | Margaret Mayo |
| A RELUCTANT WIFE | Cathy Williams |
| THE WEDDING BETRAYAL | Elizabeth Power |

## *Enchanted*™

| | |
|---|---|
| THE MIRACLE WIFE | Day Leclaire |
| TEXAS TWO-STEP | Debbie Macomber |
| TEMPORARY FATHER | Barbara McMahon |
| BACHELOR AVAILABLE! | Ruth Jean Dale |
| BOARDROOM BRIDEGROOM | Renee Roszel |
| THE HUSBAND DILEMMA | Elizabeth Duke |
| THE BACHELOR BID | Kate Denton |
| THE WEDDING DECEPTION | Carolyn Greene |

## On sale from 5th February 1999

H1 9901

*Available at most branches of WH Smith, Tesco, Asda, Martins, Borders, Easons, Volume One/James Thin and most good paperback bookshops*

# 4 FREE

## books and a surprise gift!

We would like to take this opportunity to thank you for reading this Mills & Boon® book by offering you the chance to take FOUR more specially selected titles from the Presents™ series absolutely FREE! We're also making this offer to introduce you to the benefits of the Reader Service™—

- ★ FREE home delivery
- ★ FREE gifts and competitions
- ★ FREE monthly Newsletter
- ★ Books available before they're in the shops
- ★ Exclusive Reader Service discounts

Accepting these FREE books and gift places you under no obligation to buy, you may cancel at any time, even after receiving your free shipment. Simply complete your details below and return the entire page to the address below. *You don't even need a stamp!*

**YES!** Please send me 4 free Presents books and a surprise gift. I understand that unless you hear from me, I will receive 6 superb new titles every month for just £2.30 each, postage and packing free. I am under no obligation to purchase any books and may cancel my subscription at any time. The free books and gift will be mine to keep in any case.

P9EA

Ms/Mrs/Miss/Mr.................................Initials ................................

BLOCK CAPITALS PLEASE

Surname ........................................................................................

Address ........................................................................................

..........................................................................................................

..............................................................Postcode..............................

**Send this whole page to:**
THE READER SERVICE, FREEPOST CN81, CROYDON, CR9 3WZ
(Eire readers please send coupon to: P.O. BOX 4546, DUBLIN 24.)